Nursery Crimes

This is the city of Las Fables. I work here. I'm Detective Peter Peter. I put 'em in the pumpkin shell.

Las Fables is a land of fairy tales and rhymes. Sure, it used to be made of sugar and spice, but Mother Goose flew the coop and hasn't been seen in years. Darkness has settled over the town, whiffling and galumphing down the yellow brick lanes.

When the Seven Dwarves are gunned down in the Old Woman's Shoe Bar, Detective Peter Peter and his partner Jack Horner are on the case. No matter how over the hill and far away the clues take them, they'll see that justice is served—not too hot, not too cold, but just right.

Of course it isn't just crime on Peter Peter's mind.

There's a dame named Muffet who's got him in a tizzy. And it's gonna take all of his will power to keep his heart from tumbling down after her.

Nursery Crimes

Las Fables Mystery

Devon Monk

ODD
HOUSE
PRESS

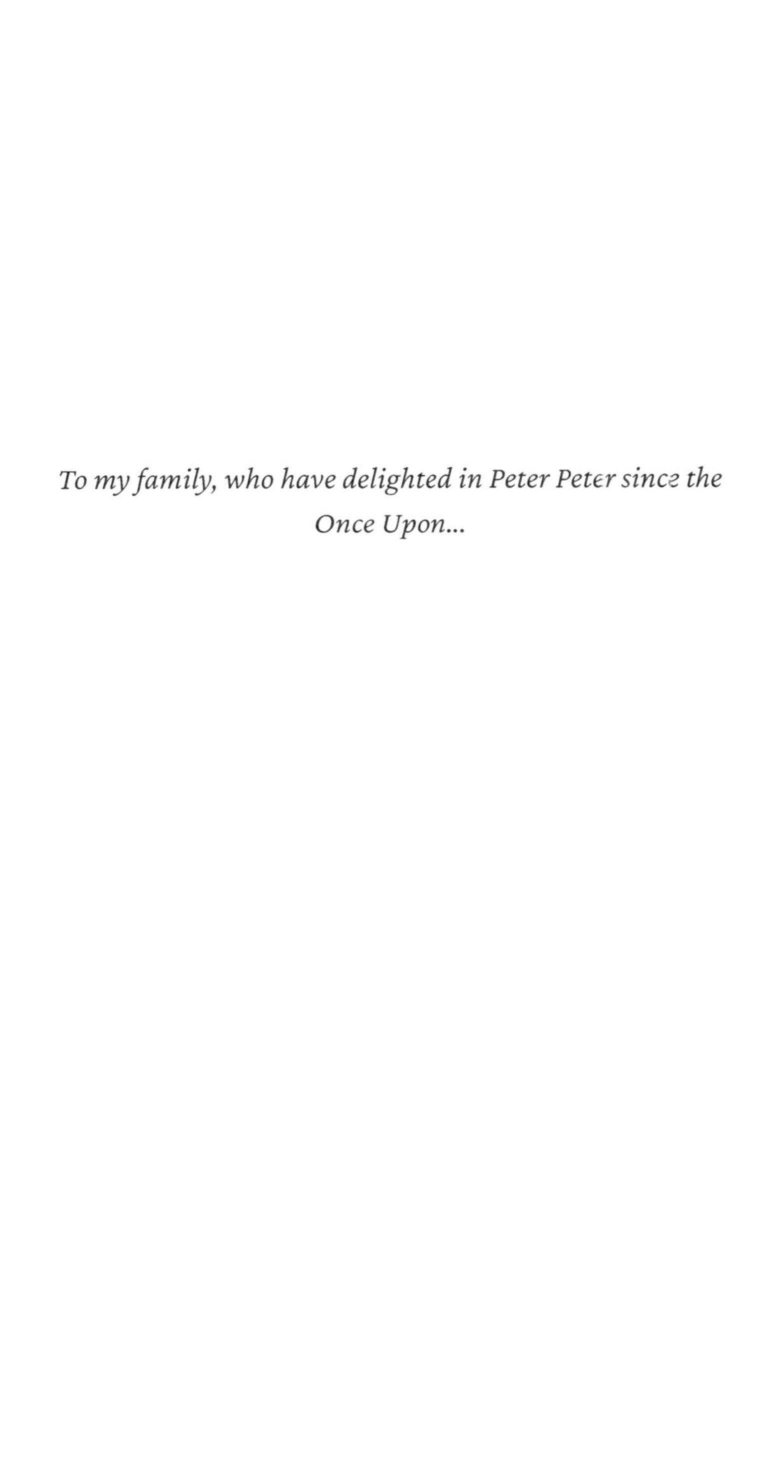

To my family, who have delighted in Peter Peter since the Once Upon...

CHAPTER 1

Most stories like this start off with a dame in a tight dress swanking into a cheap, dimly lit office. The Jill sings her siren-song to the rock-faced Jack, who's been teetering on the cliff between sobriety and blackout, just one more snort of bootleg booze and the memory of the last case he botched might finally fade into the slosh of regret.

The Detective swears he ain't gonna listen. Ain't gonna fall for the dame's sob story. He swears he ain't gonna fall down, break his crown, or come tumbling after.

Not again. Not like he has a hundred times before, his story written in permanent ink on pages no one can revise.

This story doesn't start with a Jill, or a siren song, or a granite-faced Jack.

It starts with a murder.

This is the city of Las Fables. I work here. I'm Detective Peter Peter. I put 'em in the pumpkin shell.

It was a soggy Thursday night in Las Fables, and no amount of singing was going to make the rain rain go away and come again another day.

My partner Horner and I were following up on a call.

The Little Boy who lived down the lane heard shots coming from the Old Woman's Shoe Bar. Said the Dwarves were involved.

Said there had been a fight.

Said things had gone too quiet.

Said someone was dead.

I'd heard that broken record too often lately. Assault, blood, murder, a ring-around-the-rosy of death and darkness skipping down the streets.

If I believed in scary tales, I'd say something evil was creeping through the city. A restless kind of madness that painted crooked lines between shadow and light. An evil as clear to a detective like me as the Emperor's non-existent new clothes.

Normally the things you can't see can't hurt you.

Normally imaginary boogeymen are just imaginary.

But there's nothing normal about this town.

Horner and I made the scene in three minutes flat

through a downpour that was as cold and heartless as a magic mirror.

I stepped out of my car, tugged the brim of my fedora to keep the rain out of my eyes, then parked my hands in the pockets of my trench coat.

Horner, at my side, wore a gray coat that cost half-a year's wages, his hat tipped at an angle over his eyes.

Horner was an upstanding Jack. He had a thing for clothes, interior decorating, and gourmet baking. He was level-headed, sharp-eyed, and smiled like an angel.

He also had a thumb in every pie in town. That smile and his connections had pulled the plum out of a case more than once.

The two of us had been partners since the Once Upon. There wasn't another scorcher I wanted by my side.

Except maybe Muffet, but that dame was a different kind of story. The kind that kept a guy like me up at night, wondering if I'd ever work up the nerve to ask her if I could turn the next page.

"Ready?" Horner asked.

"Or not," I said, "here we come."

We took the crooked stairs to the Shoe Bar's door in the arch of the boot. Horner flipped his collar to clear his badge. I did the same.

I pushed the door and strode into the dimly lit

Shoe. "This is the police," I said. "Everybody stay right where you are."

The boot was empty for a Thursday. A few roughs down by the toe, a few in the heel. A fluffy flock of sheep on the inner edge of the arch were playing poker.

Nobody moved.

"Gruesome," Horner said, and he wasn't talking about the sheep.

The bar averaged a fight a night, but this was different. Seven little bodies lay strewn across the floor, pick axes askew, shovels cast aside, white beards soaking up blood.

The Dwarves were dead.

CHAPTER 2

Behind the bar at the outer edge of the Shoe's arch stood the Old Woman.

She was old enough to be a contemporary of the Goose herself, but unlike The Mother, the Old Woman didn't wear glasses or a smile.

Instead, she was grim as a reaper, as broken as a bridge that had fallen down so long ago, she'd given up on pins and needles ever building it up again.

She clutched a stained rag in one hand, a dirty glass in the other, her watery gaze steady on the seven dead Dwarves.

If I didn't know better, I'd think she'd already gone to the grave without bothering to dig the hole.

To one side of the bar was the back door—a circle cut out of the boot and sewn up with cheap leather. The door was buttoned tight—with a button. It didn't look like anyone, not even the toughest in the crowd, was going to make a break for it.

All eyes were on us, and not a weapon in sight.

Plenty of witnesses.

Just how I liked it.

"Horner, call in the crime scene investigators."

"Pa, Ma, and Junior?"

I nodded. "All of them. Better get Hans and Gret Ell too."

Hans and Gret Ell were the brother-sister coroners who owned the local crematorium. They worked crime scenes with us, the messier the better. Mostly because they liked that sort of thing.

Horner strolled over to the door and pulled out his newfangled sail phone. He scribbled notes on the magic paper, then folded each one and tossed it out into the wind to find its recipient.

I strode down the insole's slant to the small tables at the heel. The group sitting there was as mismatched as the Three Blind Mice's wardrobe: a kid with a tic who I had brought in for indecent exposure—Wee Willie was his name—a tabby in dark glasses holding a fiddle in his paws, and a big hairy wolf who looked mean enough to swallow a granny whole.

"You fellows been here all night?" I asked.

They took some time to not look at me.

"How about you boys tell me exactly what just happened," I suggested. "Multiple murder isn't a private sort of affair. I know you gents saw something."

Still the silence.

"We either talk it over easy here, or I take you down to shell and give you a day or two to think about it there."

That did it. No one wanted to be incarcerated in a rotting gourd with winter coming on.

The Cat with the fiddle tapped his dark glasses with the tip of his bow. "I didn't see anything, Detective. I did hear the little guys fighting over who was gonna pay the tab though."

"Pulled out pickaxes, shovels, and hammers," Wee Willie said.

"Bunch of cheapskates," the big hairy guy added. "Like they don't save enough splitting the rent seven ways on top of owning the only gold mine in town. Screaming and yelling. Sounded like they was being eaten." His smile drew back on a rack of sharp teeth.

If Straw, Sticks, and Bricks Pigs hadn't taken the law into their own hooves back a while ago, we would have locked Big Bad away for huffing, puffing, and harassment.

"Which of them had the gun?" I asked.

Glasses clattered behind me. I threw a look at the Old Woman. She set a tumbler down on the cigarette-burned bar, picked up a new glass and rubbed it like she was hoping a genie would appear.

"Gun?" Wee Willie said. "I didn't see no gun."

The Cat tapped his shades again. "I ain't seen nothing my whole life."

"Maybe ain't none of us seen a gun." Big Bad picked at his fangs with his dewclaw. "Maybe all those little men killed each other with their bare hands."

One look at the dead Dwarves and Bad's theory fell apart. The pickaxes were thrown away from the bodies. Hammers rested against chair legs.

Maybe it had started out as a brawl, but it had ended with each dwarf taking a bullet in the head.

"That story's a bucket of holes, Bad. You sure you want to stick to it?"

"Like I said, maybe ain't none of us seen a dwarf with a gun."

"You see someone else with a gun?" I pressed.

Before Bad could answer, the door swung open. Striding across the threshold was Chuck Charming, King Cole's eldest boy and Snow White's husband. The gossip mags listed him as a verified TDH—a tall, dark, and handsome.

Of all the gin shoes in all the sin towns, he had to walk into this one.

Chuck hated the Dwarves. He'd been the butt of their jokes for years: Snow's eighth little man.

The Dwarves hated him right back. They bragged about how happy Snow had been with them in the woods. Prided themselves on being off grid with no need for royal handouts. They'd also been vocal about how proud they were that Snow had made something of herself, despite her marriage to Chuck.

Snow was the highest judge in Las Fables—the Fairest in the Land.

It wasn't just her dwarven days that didn't sit well with the royals, it was also her schooling and career they couldn't ignore, belittle, or erase.

And now, on the night of the Dwarves' murder, the royal Prince was here, in a dive boot on the wrong side of the tracks.

"Well, well." Bad sat back and licked the front of his teeth. "This just got a whole lot of interesting."

CHAPTER 3

Prince Chuck strolled across the room carrying a brown pastry box that might contain a small pie. He was graceful as a cat, as pretty as a portrait.

He moved through the space like he was made of oil paint, and we were nothing but charcoal sketches. His hair, black and full of wave, was shoulder-length dripping wet. He stopped and stared down at the pile of Dwarves.

Every eye in that boot was on the Prince. Horner gave him the up and down, then wrote something on his pad, probably the designer Chuck was wearing this season.

Chuck's expression was as blank as a jail cell wall. The only sound in the room came from sheep shuffling cards in the toe, and the rain from Chuck's coat knuckling a beat against the worn leather floor.

The TDH didn't smile, but he didn't look all that upset at the sight of the corpses either. He just licked his lips and slowly raised his gaze to the Old Woman behind me, then to me.

His eyes burned with dark joy.

"Detective." He flicked his fingers, summoning.

I joined him at the happy, grumpy, sneezy, bashful, dopey, doc, and sleepy dead.

"Prince Charming," I said.

"Who did this?"

"That's what we're here to find out."

His royal gaze swept the Shoe. "You think the killer is in the room?"

"I think I'm here to ask questions and get answers."

"But wouldn't a killer leave? To remain at the scene of a crime is just asking to be caught and found guilty."

I watched his eyes as he said that, the stingy eyes of a ruler that gave nothing away. He shifted his hold on the pastry box which, I noted, had a heart and an elegant letter Q stamped in red ink on its side. He was soaked through, either from stepping into a puddle up to his middle, or from standing in the rain for some time.

Prince Charles Charming, first in line to the throne,

standing in the rain on the wrong side of town near the Shoe Bar, waiting.

Waiting for what?

"People have all sorts of ideas of what guilt and innocence look like," I said. "What killing feels like. That a soft lie will get them out of anything a hard gun has gotten them into. Killer might be over the hill and far away by now. Or they might have stuck around to applaud until the curtain falls."

"Very poetic, Detective. Have you considered auditioning for Royal unWriter of the Realm?"

Interesting pivot, especially since that job hadn't been a real thing for years.

"Chump like me?" I said. "I don't think The Mother would let me anywhere near the stories in the Book." Not to mention the King, who had taken full control over all of our stories.

"Still, you have a way with words. Consider it. Let me know."

Not that it sounded like a bribe, but it sounded like a bribe.

"Offering to put in a good word for me if the life of a lawman doesn't work out?" I asked.

"Well," he flashed that Charming smile, "let's cross that bridge when we must, shall we?"

In other words: no. His offer was as empty as a scarecrow's brain.

"There is something you can help me with," I said.

"Do you know anyone who hated the Seven enough to want to kill them?"

The smile went brittle as a haystack full of needles. "What are you insinuating, Detective?"

I pulled a notebook out of my pocket and clicked the pen.

Casual. Just a few questions. Just the facts.

"You hear complaints from your subjects. Did anyone complain about the Dwarves? Did anyone hold grudges?"

"Everyone holds grudges. And yes, I've heard complaints. Nothing so serious I would expect murder to be the outcome. If I had suspected that, I would have called the authorities, of course."

"Of course," I agreed. "Still, I'll need a list of names and complaints."

"Contact the court recorder. All such audiences are scribed."

"Can you think of anyone who stood out?" I paused, met his gaze. "Someone who might have mentioned how much they hate the Dwarves? Someone who might feel threatened by them? Ridiculed by them?"

"No." He wasn't taking the bait but hadn't called me out on it either. Interesting.

I tucked the notebook away. "You come to this place often?"

"Occasionally. I make a point to frequent all the establishments in Las Fables."

That was news to me.

"We royals strive to be approachable for the common citizen."

News to me above and below the fold.

I was trying to picture the TDH knocking back shots with the roughs in the Shoe and just couldn't see it. Even crownless, cape-less, doing his best to blend in as a commoner with that small box still in one hand, there was nothing approachable about him.

"Has the, uh, proprietress said anything?" He gestured at the bar.

The Old Woman didn't look so good. She'd gone teary-eyed and stoop-shouldered, the glass and rag forgotten in her hands.

The murder had hit her hard. I wondered if this crime would be enough to finally bring her falling down and leave all those kids with which she didn't know what to do orphaned in the bar's matching left boot.

"Not yet," I said.

"Good proprietress," Chuck called out. "Have you any comment?"

"Screaming like a bunch of three-year-olds," she muttered. "If I wanted to hear children scream, I could stay home. Hi-hoing like they ruled the place."

She pointed one knobby finger at the pile of

bodies. "Look at the mess they made. Who's going to clean this up? Who's going to take care of this? You, your royal Charming?"

Her gaze flicked to the box. "Your mother?" She gave a short laugh. "When have your kind ever done anything with your own hands? When have you cared about what happens to us little people?"

Chuck frowned and even that looked good on him. "All people in the realm are my concern. If I can be of assistance, Old Woman, bring your petition before my father, the King, and we will see that your needs are served. As for my mother, she sends her regards."

He strode past me and placed the box on the bar.

The Old Woman ignored it, and ignored him.

"What's with the box?" I asked the Prince.

Having gotten no response from the Old Woman, he turned my way. "The Queen sends tarts to various businesses to let them know how much she cares."

In a quieter voice, he said, "I expect you will keep me fully informed on this investigation. It is a most distressing turn of events for both myself and my wife, Princess Snow."

I believed half of that. Snow, at least, was going to be heartbroken.

"Do you want an escort home?" I asked. "Someone to go over the event with Snow? I could assign Muffet to stay with her."

"No," he said. "I alone, the love of her life, will tell her this most terrible news."

Dramatic. Like I didn't see enough of that in my job.

Chuck spun with enough force to make his coat wing. He stepped over the dwarves. Didn't even have the decency to look down at them as he strode out of the Shoe, just an actor closing a scene.

Not even a drop of blood dirtied his expensive shoes.

Horner caught my gaze and raised one eyebrow.

I shook my head.

I knew what he was asking: Shouldn't we take Chuck in on suspicion?

Chuck hated the Seven, that was no secret. It was also no secret that people the royalty didn't approve of had been removed from this city, erased from the Book.

Remember ol' Gawking Ghoul who proved the King a fool? Of course you don't. He was tossed out of town, his story unwritten from the Book. He faded away. Became a Nothing, less than a dream, thinner than a Nary Tale on the winter wind.

Tonight, for Snow's sake, I would cut Chuck some slack.

Tomorrow would be a different story.

CHAPTER 4

The Three Bears lumbered into the Shoe Bar to record the details of the crime scene while the clues were not too hot, not too cold, but just right. Ma and Pa took notes, and Junior snapped pictures of the entire gruesome scene.

"The Bears? You called the Bears?" The Old Woman's voice cracked like cockleshells. "What's next? Lions and tigers and flying monkeys? The mess they'll make! The mess."

"The Bears are here to record the crime scene, Ma'am," I said. "They won't make a mess."

The Bears sniffed at the bodies, then Ma and Pa Bear did a thorough sniff around the Shoe as Junior bagged up the pickaxes, shovels, and hammers.

I turned back to Big Bad and the others at the

table. "You said the Dwarves argued about the bar tab. Is that all you heard?"

"That's all."

"You didn't hear the gunfire?"

"Sure, I heard the gun," Bad said. "Everybody heard that."

Willie nodded. Or at least I assume Wee Willie's jittering was agreement. He was on his way to a full-blown fit. The Cat just grinned, his teeth cutting a crescent moon across his furry face.

"You're telling me you heard seven shots but didn't see who did the shooting?"

"Here's the thing, Detective," Bad said. "Maybe figuring out who did the shooting is your job, not mine."

"Sounds about right," I agreed. "Horner, take these gentlemen into the station. We'll need their full statement."

Horner sauntered over. "You heard the man. Get a move on, gents."

Big Bad hollered and made threats, Wee Willie winked uncontrollably and cussed a streak. The Cat smiled and faded away until he was nothing but a handful of stripes and black sunglasses hovering in the air.

Horner got them all moving, even the invisible Cat, and escorted them out to the car.

"Peter," Pa Bear rambled over to me. "There's no

gun. Not that we can find."

"You sure?"

He snorted. "Sniff for yourself if you don't believe me."

I did believe him but started a slow search of the place anyway. The Shoe might be old and shabby, but it had been swept recently. There was no dirt on the floor. No bloody footprints, no gun waiting to be found under a table.

"Don't think we have room in the car for the sheep," Horner said, tapping on the table I was looking under.

"Leave them alone; they'll go home." I straightened. "We'll know where to find them."

Sure enough, the sheep were folding their cards and divvying the chips. They hopped out of their chairs and single-filed it out the door, wagging their tails behind them.

That left me, Horner, the Old Woman, and the Bears.

"What do you think?" I asked Horner.

"Doesn't sit right with me," he said. "We're supposed to believe one of the Dwarves was packing, plugged his brothers over the rent payment, killed himself and, what, the gun disappeared?"

"I've never known a Seven to use a gun," I said. "They've been together since the Once Upon. Why this? Why now?"

Horner ran his thumb over the edge of his notebook and glanced at the door. "You sure you don't want me to bring Chuck in for questioning?"

"We'll get statements from the other witnesses first, then we'll visit the royals."

"How do you think Snow's going to take it?"

"Like a queen." Publicly, at least. I knew Snow would be broken up, no matter how cool and composed she pretended to be.

"And the Book?" he asked.

That was a problem.

The Dwarves' death would change Las Fables in a big way. Most deaths left a hole in our stories, a hole that could sometimes be filled with a different character or rhyme.

There were a lot of Jacks around town—the Nimble, the Sprat, the Giant Killer. One Jack might be able to fill in for the other.

But the Seven Dwarves were fundamental, irreplaceable. They were a foundational part of Snow's life and story. A foundational part of the royal's story.

Rewriting—or erasing them from the Book completely—would take the approval of the King, and the King hadn't approved of a story change in years.

But no one could ignore that the Seven were dead. Snow's and Prince Charming's stories were about to change. Permanently.

I didn't know what that would do to our town.

That was just one problem we had on our hands.

The other problem? Big Bad was right. The Dwarves possessed the only gold mine in Las Fables. They owned a lot of hill and dale. Only the Three Pigs brothers and the royal family were as rich as the Seven.

Taking out the Seven created an open invitation for a power grab. It offered a ripe opportunity to rise up and become a big story in this little town.

There were plenty of shady characters waiting in the margins for a chance like this.

That much gold, land, and foundational story were enough to make even innocent farmers' wives sharpen their carving knives.

I nodded toward the Old Woman, who was the last witness we needed to interview here. "We'll deal with the Book," I told Horner, "and the Dwarves' story once Mother Goose finds out they're dead."

"If she finds out," Horner added.

I winced, but yeah, that was the gamble. We hadn't heard from the Goose

in more years than there were bottles of beer on the wall. She'd all but flown the coop and left Las Fables to its own devices.

She had left King Cole the key to the Vault where the Book was kept, giving him full control of the Book.

"Goose or no Goose," I amended, "we'll deal with the Dwarves' stories."

"You'll deal with everything," the Old Woman said as we stepped up to the bar.

"What's that, Ma'am?"

"You'll deal with everything now. The nightmare, the mess. It's not my job to clean this up. I did my part." She scrubbed another clean glass. "I have a business to run."

Horner nodded sympathetically. "We'll be closing the bar while we finish with the crime scene. I think you'd best stay home for a few days."

"Home in a shoe full of screaming brats? No thank you, Detective. I'm staying here."

It was strange for her to choose the Doc Martin of death over her own home. The Bears would need at least twenty-four hours to gather pictures, dust for prints, and scour for clues.

The Old Woman was either being stubborn or she was afraid to leave the bar.

"What did you see tonight?" I asked. "Can you tell us what happened?"

"Now you're going to harass an old woman after you've closed her business? I can sue, you know. I have rights. Even an old woman has rights. Hi-ho."

"You do have rights." Horner rested his hand on the bar near hers, quietly offering support. "We can provide you with an attorney and, if you want, counseling, therapy, even papers to file for loss of income from the investigation. But we do need a statement, Ma'am."

"I don't have anything to say to you," she grumbled, resisting his charm. "This shoe fits me fine, and I'm wearing it."

"Sure." Horner leaned an elbow on the bar and flashed his angel smile. It didn't make him a TDH, but there was a sincerity to it, a good-heartedness that always seemed to get through to people.

Jack was a stand-up guy who wanted to help people. It showed.

The Old Woman's expression softened. "I'm listening."

"This is your place of business," he said. "We understand that. We don't want to put you in a bind. How about you come out from behind the bar and have a seat while we talk? I bet you've been on your feet all day."

She blinked at him as if blinded by starlight. "It's been a long time," she admitted. "So long. The nightmare, you know."

Horner, unlike me, was good with people. Easy.

He extended his hand. "A very difficult night. You can tell us all about it if you'd like."

She reached for him, comforted, ready to spill the beans.

But before she touched his hand, the door slammed open.

CHAPTER 5

Hans and Gret Ell sauntered into the joint, body bags slung over their shoulders.

The siblings wore shiny black coats, gloves, and breeches, all tight as a glass slipper on the wrong sister's foot. Their hair was dyed bright—Hans' green as a magic bean, Gret's red as a riding hood.

They'd given up on their childhood candy habit since that run in with the witch out in the Tulgey Wood and were now a muscular, pale-skinned, dark-eyed pair.

These babes in the woods hadn't laid down and died so much as gotten down with death.

The Bears gave them a paw's-up, and the Ells waved back.

Without batting an eye at the pool of blood or the little men soaking it up, the brother and sister got busy toe-tagging, body-bagging, and piling dwarves onto stretchers.

They whistled while they worked which was, once I thought about it, apropos.

The grunt and squeak of Hans and Gret dwarfing the stretchers seemed too loud in the Shoe. Silver flashes from Junior's camera flickered across the boot like static in a wool sock, and just like that, the moment for the Old Woman telling Jack everything flickered out and was gone.

"You should leave," the Old Woman whispered.

"Ma'am," I said. "We'll still need your statement. Why don't we go down to the station and give the Bears and the Ells room to work?"

"You want my statement? Fine. They deserved it. All Seven of them deserved each shot."

Horner shook his head, but clicked his pen and took notes.

"You're saying they deserved to die?" I asked, doing my best to keep it easy like Jack. "Why's that?"

Her eyes had taken on a faraway look, her head tipped like she heard something coming this way.

Outside, the rain drummed against the shabby roof and the north wind did blow. Beyond the sound of rain, beyond the whistling of the Ells pushing Dwarves through the door, I caught the softest whiffle.

But it couldn't be a whiffle, not in Las Fables. The only creature that whiffled didn't exist.

The wind shifted and the sound of someone humming a tune about hushed babies, mockingbirds, and pretty broken toys filled the air.

The humming grew louder, and a man shouldered past the Ells who had just finished removing the Dwarves.

Athletic, blond, with eyes so blue they shone neon across the smoky room, Boy Blue carried a crate of whiskey in his arms. He got one look at Horner, and the lullaby died on his lips.

"Jack?" he asked.

Boy Blue was a jazz musician and the eldest of the Old Woman's brood. He was hardworking and honest and had done everything he could to keep his siblings happy and fed.

He was the only thing that had kept the story of the bar and their family from falling into the Book's margins or gutter.

Pa Bear rose up on his hind legs, eight hundred pounds of shag wall. "Crime scene," he growled. "No citizens allowed."

"It's okay, Pa," I said. "It's her boy, Blue."

Pa dropped to all fours and gave a hard sniff, confirming his scent. "Sorry, Blue. Go ahead."

Blue set the crate on the floor, his gaze still on Horner. He started toward him, the brass horn hooked on his belt shining like a lucky penny.

Horner brushed a hand over his hair and cleared

his throat, looking uncommonly flustered. "Blue," he said, his voice a certain kind of husky.

Yeah, there was something between them. I assumed they wanted to keep it on the down low. Horner had never come right out and told me about it, and I respected his privacy enough not to ask.

Yet.

"Hey, Jack," Blue said with a smile. "Finally come by for that drink?"

Horner smiled back, then shook his head. "Here on business." He waved at the floor. "Like Pa said, crime scene. The Dwarves were killed."

Blue stilled and looked around. "What do you mean? Here?"

"Yes."

"Dead? Who?"

"All of them."

He glanced at his mother. "How? Who would…" His gaze ticked down to the little brown box with the heart stamp on the bar. It was out of place—a royal treat in the middle of a common tragedy.

"How?" he asked. "Why would anyone? Why here? Now?"

"Shot," I said, answering his first question before knocking down the next. "We don't know who. Don't know why. Not yet. We need a statement from your mother, and you, if you'll give it."

He considered the Old Woman who was avoiding looking at any of us.

"Mom?"

"Rotten brats," she muttered.

He paused, weighing his choices. "I think she'll...I think I can bring her to the station to give a statement."

"Broth without bread. You don't deserve bread."

He nodded absently as if he'd heard her say that all his life.

"But not tonight. She needs some time. All Seven? Gone?" That was for Horner, who nodded gravely.

"Can I bring her by the station in the morning? She's...well, she's better in the morning."

It wasn't the way we did things, but the Dwarves weren't getting any deader. We had Bad, Willie, and the Cat to interview tonight.

If they gave us enough to go on, the Old Woman's testimony would serve as corroboration.

"Tomorrow will work," I said.

He exhaled, gratitude all over him. "Thank you. I really appreciate this. I'll get her home and settled, then be there in the morning."

He approached his mother and placed his hands over hers until she put the glass and rag down on the bar.

"Time to go home," he said quietly.

"I'll sleep with corpses before I spend another minute with you brats."

"Come home, Mom. There's nothing more to do here. You know I'll keep them quiet at home."

"I wish you'd never been born. All of you. I wish you were dead. Dead as the Dwarves."

Horner took half a step forward, then stopped himself. Frowned.

Blue didn't let go of her hands. "Sure." His expression was what hope looked like when its kneecaps had been broken for the last time. "Let's just go home now."

The Old Woman's rhyme said she had too many kids and didn't know what to do about them. The way it was written, it said she'd taken to whipping them all soundly before sending them to bed.

Her kids were all older now, but the Old Woman still knew how to dole out the hurt.

And sure, her story was written hard, but she had made no effort to ease it in some way, to make good of it, like Snow had made good of being "Fairest in the Land."

She could have whipped her kids up a pie, could have whipped some cream, or even whipped them at a game of cards.

We were all tied to our own stories. Stories we had little hope of rewriting. But that didn't mean we had to be our worst because of them.

The Old Woman glared at Horner and me.

"I want this clean by tomorrow," she ordered. "I'm not cleaning this mess. Not cleaning anyone's mess again."

"We'll do what we can, Ma'am," I said. "Get some rest."

Blue tossed me a grateful look and guided her out from behind the bar toward the door. "See you later, Detectives."

"Blue?" Horner said.

Blue might have had hope in those eyes, might have had shame.

"If...if you come by the station tonight, I'll...we'll be there."

"What about me?" the Old Woman groused. "Doesn't anybody care what I do? Where I go? Doesn't anyone care about me?"

"Of course we care, Ma'am," Horner said. "We're looking forward to you coming by tomorrow. You've had a long, difficult day."

"That's right," she grumbled. "I stand on my feet all day to put broth on the table for ungrateful brats who tear the house apart. Who takes care of me? Who looks after me?"

She tugged her hand free of Blue's grip and turned on Horner.

"You don't how hard it is to be a mother. My

story," she pounded her bony chest. "Nothing but pain. What do you have? Plum pie."

She drew herself up. "Good boy," she spat. "Easy for you. Not me. Never me. I did what I had to do. It's all going to be different now."

"Come on, Mom." Blue caught her elbow and steered her toward the door, not quite meeting Horner's gaze.

They slipped out of the Shoe and into the storm.

I pulled a cigarette from my pocket to give Horner some time to stare after him.

"That thing between Blue and you?"

"There's no thing."

I waited.

Horner sighed. "It's personal, Peter. Nothing to do with my story or duty."

Horner had been there for me, and I'd been there for him. I knew I could trust him at his word.

"Tell me about the thing you don't have with Blue some time," I said. "I'll buy the coffee."

"How about when we're not up to our knees in dead dwarves?" He lit a match and held it steady for me. I leaned in to light my cigarette.

I exhaled smoke while taking one last look around.

Something about the whole thing stank. There was more to this story than I was being told.

Why the Seven?

Why now?

Why here?

"Ma, Pa, Junior," I said. "Let us know when you wrap this up."

They grunted, one too hard, one too soft, and one just right.

"Might need that coffee quick as a candlestick," Horner said. "We have three witnesses to question tonight."

"Good. One of them knows who had their finger on the trigger." I flipped up my collar and adjusted my hat. "I want that killer off the yellow bricks of my city before the morning bells are ringing."

"Ding, dang, dong," Horner agreed.

My partner and I ducked out into the dark and stormy night and jogged to the car.

CHAPTER 6

The way I figure it, sevens don't always come up lucky. First it was the mining accident that forced two of the Dwarves to change their names to Lefty and Limpy, then it was the shooting at the Old Woman's Shoe Bar that left them all dead.

Luck in Las Fables has a way of teeter-tottering. Sometimes it's up, sometimes it's down. Too bad the Dwarves' luck had tottered out.

I pulled up to the station and cut the engine. Horner and I were silent a moment while we took a gander at the fellow leaning against the station stairwell.

Chic Ken Little was a greasy little guy in a yellow zoot suit. He was chewing gum and staring at us like his train was thinking-it-could all the way up to the top of Big Rock Candy Mountain.

His oversized hat kept the blocky camera hung around his scrawny neck dry from the pouring rain.

I didn't have to guess why he was hanging around the station on a night like tonight. The Sixpence Slinger's loud-mouthed reporter had a thing for crime: He liked it a little too much.

I had a thing for the loud-mouthed reporter: I hated him. If I ever found a reason to throw his story out of the Book, I would be in Judge White's courtroom faster than a rip can winkle.

"Want to take the back way in?" Horner asked.

"And miss a chance to tell him to breeze off?" I opened the door and strode into the steady drizzle and up the stairs.

Little pushed his hat back, sticking out a nose that had taken so many hits, it was as crooked as a witch's fist. He lifted the camera and popped a flash-white shot of me and Horner who was escorting the witnesses up the stairs.

"Beat bricks, Little," I said. "No loitering." I took the steps two at a time, leaving him behind.

"Heard the Dwarves got gunned down." He had a raw-lemon voice, uncomfortably sour, like he'd spent all his day screaming at the sky.

"That's quite a hit to your reputation, Peter Peter," he screeched. "All Seven in one blow. Tragic. Care to comment on how the force failed to stop such a brutal crime? Care to comment on the recent rise in crime? Care to comment on how the citizens of Las Fables are in danger while the department—your department—is woefully inadequate and unprepared to handle it?”

I stopped and looked way, way down at him, both from a physical standpoint and a moral one.

“No. Do you want to comment on the lurid lies you print that have ruined people's lives, Chic?”

His beady eyes narrowed. He hated his first name.

When my ex-wife Peggy worked for Chic at the paper, he'd had his eye on her. He'd tipped Peggy off about Bo Peep spending too much time with the King behind the Queen's back.

He'd sent Peggy to the field that day to interview Bo Peep, saying it would be the story of the century. Instead, it became the crime of the century.

Peggy had killed an innocent Humpty egg for a scoop on a royal scandal that had long ago faded away.

But the law was the law, and she'd broken it into more pieces than poor Dumpty. I'd had to bring her in. Just like my story says, I had a wife and couldn't keep her. I locked her in the shell on murder charges.

Peggy might not be pure or innocent, but Chic was filthy as the devil's sooty brother.

“If you remain on these steps, Chic,” I said, “I will take you in for loitering, harassment, and public nuisance.”

I gave him a gravedigger's stare, and he shoveled it right back. That little engine of his was still chugging to couple two thoughts together. Looked like he was going to open his big mouth.

Good. I had a strong need to punch something.

"Take a leap, Chic," Horner called out from the station doors. "You don't want to push your luck tonight. Not with us. Not now."

"Coward." Chic snapped, crackled, and popped his gum. "I'll say hello to your wife for you next time I visit her in shell, Detective Peter. She likes it when a real man stops by and takes care of her needs, if you know what I mean."

Horner had walked down to stand beside me, and he clamped his hand on my shoulder.

"Let it go, Boss. He's just squawking at a falling sky."

"You have something you want to say to me?" Chic sneered. "Something you want to do to me, maybe?"

The film camera *clack-clacked* as he lined up a new shot. He was pushing for a scene. Pushing me to lose my cool and give him a headline because headlines and ruining lives were the only things he cared about.

I refused to give him a drop of ink. I leaned in closer, the rain off the brim of my hat dribbling down to soak his camera. "Run off and play, little chicken. I have work to do."

"I'm watching you!" Little shouted. "Don't think I

don't know what you do. Don't think I won't expose you."

Those threats were as empty as Hubbard's cupboard. I had a case that needed me, a murderer to find. One fowl mouth wasn't going to stop me from doing my job.

I walked up into the station and let the familiar low chatter welcome me.

Tom Stout, an upstanding officer with the solid build of a farmer's son, nodded as I passed.

The rest of the officers sitting at the other desks were busy reading reports, writing reports, or reporting on reports.

I made my way to my office in the corner of the room, walls made of glass between me and the bullpen.

Horner followed me to the door.

"Coffee?" he asked.

"Blacker the better."

I backstroked out of my coat, and hung it and my hat on the rack to drip dry. My office door was open, and I kept it that way.

I sat at my desk and listened to the clamor of the living around me: quiet arguments, papers shuffling, keys clacking, the pop and snort of a bad joke pitched, received, and knocked out of the park.

This was the jazz beat of my life: work to be done, cases to be solved, miles to go to keep Las Fables safe.

These were the people who helped me see that it was done right.

Still, there were quiet moments when I wondered if law and order, story and duty were all there was to life. Wondered if there was more than going through the motions strictly by the Book. Wondered if I'd ever find someone to fill the sleepy hollows of my days.

The image of Detective Muffet filtered through my mind, bringing with it a drum roll of memories. Plenty of the good times in my life had been made better by her being in them.

If I had guts, I'd ask her out. See if our stories matched. See if a dame like her would ever say yes to a chump like me.

But somehow it was never the right time to ask.

Story and duty. Those were my guiding stars. It was the only way a hard-working Joe could keep his life straight.

My story and duty were to solve a murder.

I blew out a breath and shook my head. Singing the blues about a dame would have to wait.

All seven of the Dwarves were dead. They'd only left behind one person who'd need a handkerchief at their funeral: Snow White.

Maybe having one person who cared enough was plenty for a life. Plenty for seven lives.

I dragged a pad of paper to the center of the desk and started a list.

The Cat, Wee Willie, and Bad didn't fit the profile of a multiple murderer but I put them on the list anyway. The sheep didn't have enough brains between them to fire a gun, and the Old Woman had really tumbled down the hill in the last few years. She seemed to be in even worse shape than the sheep.

That took care of everyone in the bar.

If the Bears couldn't come up with something more to go on—like the gun—we'd have to find the killer the hard way: by questioning every Jack, Jill, and fast-footed cookie in Las Fables.

Making a list of who hated the Dwarves and checking it twice would take most of the night. The Seven were well known, but not well-liked.

The Three Pigs had never gotten along with them. The Seven had a long-standing rivalry with Chuck Charming.

We'd followed up on rumors that the Dwarves were laundering money for the Fairy Godfather. Never could prove it, but if it were true, the Fairy might have his wand shoved up in this mess.

He, of all the people in the city, had the power and connections to kill the Seven and make sure no one said a peep about it.

Well, he and any of the royal family, I supposed.

I worked methodically, noting possibilities, tracking connections, sketching motives.

Loud voices broke my concentration. I rubbed at

the headache starting behind my eyes and assessed the commotion.

Horner and Boy Blue were escorting the Old Woman across the station toward me.

She demanded her rights, pointing at officers accusingly, and muttered nonsense about nightmares and hi-hoing.

Horner eased her into the chair next to Tom Stout's desk.

Tom smiled and motioned toward the teapot he kept there. It was short and stout, which meant he had to stand up and do the here's the handle and here's the spout routine.

I don't make the tea rules, but all that dancing is the reason I drink coffee.

At the end of the song and dance, he poured her a cup. That seemed to settle her mood.

Horner and Blue strode to my office.

"Boss." Horner dropped an evidence bag onto my desk.

An evidence bag that contained a gun.

CHAPTER 7

I pushed back from the desk and looked up at my partner. "Talk."

"Blue has something he wants to tell you," Horner said. "In private."

Blue wiped his mouth then stared at his boots.

"That so?" I asked Blue.

He glanced at Horner. "Stay with her?"

"I'll be right out here where you can see us." His voice softened. "Just tell Peter what you told me."

"What about me?" the Old Woman yelled from Stout's desk halfway across the station. "Who's going to talk to me? Who's going to listen to me? The nightmare! I have rights!"

Horner gave me a look and stepped out.

"Have a seat, Blue."

He shook his head. "I just want to get this over with."

"Okay. Talk."

He took a breath, his shoulders going back, his stance relaxing. He was a musician, and a damn fine one. He knew how to face an audience and bare his soul.

"The gun belongs to my mother. I found it in the holster under her shawl after I took her home. It didn't have any bullets in it, but she always keeps it loaded. Always."

His neon blue gaze was searching for a shoreline through the fog of his pain. It landed on me, so I guided him in.

"She did it, Detective. My mother shot the Dwarves."

He laced fingers together on top of his head, as if he were the one surrendering, a tide of tears rising.

"She never liked the Dwarves. They were too loud, too short, too much like her kids. Too much like me and my siblings. She's our mother, you know? She never hurt us in a permanent way. But she shot the Seven. I know she must have."

"You're turning in your own mother?"

"Yeah," he whispered. "Yes."

There could be a lot of motives for his visit. He could have shot the Dwarves. Used his mother's gun, cut out of the joint quick, then strolled back with the whiskey, innocent as a mittenless kitten.

He could be accusing her to get the old lady off his back after years of abuse.

Was Blue that kind of Jack?

I didn't think so. But I needed cold, hard facts to prove it either way.

"Has your mother always carried a gun?"

"Just the last few weeks. I never thought she'd use it. But when we got home, she was threatening...my siblings. They're pretty rowdy, loud. We argue, I mean everyone argues sometimes."

He swallowed and dropped his hands, then didn't seem to know what to do with them.

"Now she's followed through on her threats...I had to...I can't believe she followed through. It could have been us. It could have been."

So, his theory was the Dwarves had been rowdy in the Shoe Bar, reminding her of her kids. The Old Woman had snapped and decided to give her new weapon a test run.

The witnesses and the Old Woman herself had said the Seven were arguing, making a lot of noise.

Blue dashed fingers across his eyes and wiped them on his jeans.

"What if she had followed through on her other threats? No one should live like that. Wondering when a gun's going to be aimed at their head.

"I'm the oldest. It's my place to look after my siblings. So that's why I'm here. That's what I'm doing."

I tapped the arm of my chair, thinking. "If she did this, your mother will be locked away. Do you understand how serious that is?"

He nodded.

"She has a right to an attorney, and one will be provided for her if she needs one. But Blue? Chances are you'll have to testify against her."

"I know. I mean, I'm the one who found her gun on her. Telling you. Reporting this. Seven. All Seven." He bit his lip. "Will Judge White will go easier on her if she turns herself in?"

"White's the Fairest in the Land. Her personal feelings about the Dwarves won't get in the way of justice being served. Your mom will get a fair trial."

"Good. I'll testify if I have to. Can she...Can I take her home tonight?"

"No. We'll hold her for questioning." At his look, I said, "She'll be comfortable here. Safe." I didn't add that he and his siblings might be safer with her here too.

I picked up the evidence bag and motioned for him to follow me. It was time to get this over with.

"Jack," I said, stopping at Stout's desk. "Tom."

I turned to the Old Woman and held up the bag. "Is this your gun, Ma'am?"

"So, what if it is?" she said. "I need protection working in that ratty boot. Blue isn't gonna look after me. Nobody's gonna look after me. All those drunks and bums and dwarves. The nightmare. Making messes. Making noise. Making trouble."

"Did you shoot the Dwarves, Ma'am?" I asked.

She sealed her lips righty-tighty.

I placed the bag next to the little teapot. "You have the right to remain silent," I began quietly.

"Right?" she demanded. "What right does an old woman like me got? The right to live a story I hate? The nightmare everywhere I look? Or maybe I have the right to do what everyone knows should have been done years ago."

"What should have been done?" Horner asked.

She clammed up again, so I put my hand on her thin arm. "We'll need you to stay the night, Ma'am. You have the right to an attorney."

"You're taking me to shell?"

"You are being charged with multiple murders."

She laughed, big and full-throated. "You call that a crime? Killing those nasty little men?"

"Yes, Ma'am. I do. And so will the judge."

"But I did what..." Something bright and clever shifted in her eyes. "Will I be alone in shell? No kids? No cleaning? No mess? No trouble? No noise?"

"If you cannot afford an attorney," I went on, "one will be provided for you."

"How long could I get for killing all Seven?"

"Life, Ma'am."

"Solitary confinement..." The words tumbled with wonder.

"I did it! It was my idea. I killed the Dwarves. Ask Blue. He knows. Ask any of the brats. I'm guilty. I said I'd do it, and it worked out just like I said it would. Only me. No one but me."

Something about her confession didn't ring true, but a confession had to be treated as truth unless proved otherwise.

Blue sobbed, a small choking sound. He looked like he was one huff, one puff, from his whole house blowing down.

Horner rested his hand on Blue's back. Blue leaned toward him a bit, though his gaze never left his mother.

"I'll take her to processing," Horner offered.

"No need," I said. "Stout can come with me. You stay here and take care of Blue."

Horner raised his eyebrows.

I said what I said, but I clarified: "Get his statement. See that he understands the process."

Yeah, we all knew how to do our jobs, but even if there wasn't anything between him and Blue, Horner was a better man than I was to help Blue through the shock of seeing a person he loved hauled away on criminal charges.

I'd been through that with my ex-wife. Horner had been the one to help me then. I couldn't have asked for anyone better.

Blue needed Horner right now.

Stout and I led the Old Woman to a quiet room, took her full confession and, just like my story said, I put her in the pumpkin shell.

By the time I was done, the station had emptied out, Horner and Blue were nowhere to be seen, and night outside had gone thick as Georgie's pudding pie.

Story and duty. Two guiding stars that kept a Joe on the straight and narrow. It could just as easily lead a fool off a cliff.

Unanswered questions chased round my mulberry bush: Why had the Old Woman snapped, tonight of all nights?

Why had Chuck Charming gone to a bar in a cold downpour when he should have been home in a warm castle with Snow?

And why hadn't the Cat, Wee Willie, or Big Bad ratted out the Old Woman when they'd had the chance?

The whole thing stunk worse than a giant's armpit.

I pulled on my coat and hat, then walked through the quiet station to the stairs outside.

Clouds covered the night sky. Down had come the

rain and washed the spiders out, shining the edges of the street like a hard candy gloss.

If the Old Woman's admission were true, there was another story in the Book that needed rewriting, one even a chump like me could imagine:

> *There was an old woman,*
> *ran a bar in a shoe.*
> *She was fed up with her kids,*
> *and the little dwarves too.*
> *If the dwarves had shut up,*
> *and gone mining instead,*
> *They'd have gold in their pockets,*
> *instead of lead.*

The wind shifted and a burble galumphed down the street. I turned toward the strange sound. Just when I spotted a shadow, the wind blew it out like a birthday candle.

Silence again. A chill hopscotched down my spine, hit home, turned and hopped back up again.

The Old Woman had said a lot in her confession. A lot about dwarves and riches and poor people with nothing. She blamed the kids for everything that had gone wrong in her life.

I'd expected that.

What I hadn't expected was her mentioning a nightmare, then refusing to talk about it. What I hadn't expected was her begging for solitary confinement.

There was only one reason I knew for a person to want to be locked away from the world like that and left all alone—fear.

I lit a cigarette and breathed in the smoke. There might be evil on these streets, but not for long. Not if I had anything to say about it.

CHAPTER 8

Friday morning, six o'clock. Horner and I were catching breakfast a couple blocks from the station at Paddy Cake's diner.

Paddy himself swung by our table. "Black coffee and fried pumpkin for Peter Peter, water and plum pie for Horner. No Muffet today?"

"Not today," I said.

Paddy was still standing there, all in his place with a big smile on his bright shiny face. "So, when are you asking her out on a date, Detective Peter?"

"Who?" I asked, even though I knew exactly who he was talking about.

"Who? Why, Muffet, of course. I know you're sweet on her."

"Who says I'm sweet on her?" I threw a glare at my

partner because I was pretty sure I knew the answer to that question too.

Horner grinned and leaned back, offering me no help.

"No one had to tell me," the baker man said. "The two of you are like the owl and the pussycat. The dish and the spoon. Mark it with an M for Muffet and me. We're all waiting for one of you to make a move. Aren't we, Jack?"

"No comment," he said with a straight face, the traitor.

I cut a bite of fried pumpkin. "How about we keep my private life off the menu?"

"Too late, Detective. We're all an open book here, aren't we?" Paddy laughed at that tired old joke and headed back to the kitchen.

I chewed the fried pumpkin and washed it down with coffee, not really tasting either. "Wonder where Paddy got the idea about Muffet and me."

"According to him, he just had to use his eyes."

"Or maybe someone on the force has been talking. Who do you suppose would be talking about Muffet and me, Partner?"

Horner huffed a laugh. "You're being awful defensive about something that isn't a something. But I haven't said a thing about either of you. Paddy's just a jolly old elf today."

I grunted and changed the subject. "How's Blue? Did you get him home okay?"

The morning edition of the Sixpence Slinger was folded behind the salt and pepper.

The multiple murder splashed across the front page, Chic's article accusing the force of failing to protect the Seven. He claimed Las Fables needed new leadership in law enforcement. Claimed I should step down.

The picture of Horner and me outside the station made us look serious and defeated.

The picture got it half right. We were serious, but we were nowhere near defeated.

"Blue got home fine. He's good." Horner shoveled a bite of pie into his mouth. "Good enough," he amended.

"He and some of his siblings are going to work together to keep the bar open. They're old enough to be out of the shoe now anyway. You buy the Old Woman's confession?"

"Nope."

He sighed. "Me either." He set his fork down next to the barely-eaten pie and frowned.

"Talk," I said around another bite of my boring breakfast.

"Why were the Seven fighting over the tab? They have more money than half of Las Fables. Suddenly a few pints of beer are too expensive? And why was

Chuck in the neighborhood? Hard to believe he was just wandering the streets."

"If the Old Woman shot the Seven," I added, "was she working alone? Which means we have to ask, is Blue on the level? He'd gain the most by the Old Woman going to shell, leaving the bar behind for him and his sibs."

"Cat, Willie, Bad are loose ends too," he said, not denying my point.

"Yeah," I agreed. "This confession tub's sinking before it can float."

The bell over the door rang out, and Detective Miss Muffet strode into the joint.

My heartbeat skipped a rope.

Spider traps the size of Horner's thumb lined a strap across her chest. She wore black breeches, shirt, and heavy boots. Her golden hair was tied back in a single braid and capped with a red beret.

She was the most gorgeous thing I'd seen in my life.

Cans of insect repellent swung from both hips as she scanned the diner looking for me.

"Boss," she said, clanking my way. "We have a problem."

Paddy threw me a wink from behind the diner counter, then gave a thumb's up.

I gulped the last of the coffee and tossed few coppers on the table.

"Let's take it outside," I said.

Ever since that spider episode, Muffet had an itchy trigger finger. I didn't know when Paddy had last bombed for bugs and didn't want to take chances in a diner full of civilians.

Muffet rattled her cans out the door, Horner and me right behind her.

The rain had let up, leaving the city looking fresh and clean. Muffet looked good, too. She was nearly my height, built like a dream, and smart as a whip.

She was a hell of a cop, too, and could hold her own against anything Las Fables threw at her: spider, wolf, or wicked step-witch.

Any person in this town would be lucky to have her.

Paddy's talk about dishes and spoons and owls and pussycats made me wonder what sort of lug Muffet was looking for. Was there a chance it was a lug like me?

"What's the problem?" I asked.

"Hostage situation," she said. "The Dwarves' place. A gang. They're calling themselves the Sins. They've got Snow White."

My blood chilled.

"What do they want?"

"A woman to deliver the Book to them, or they'll kill Snow."

The Book. Of course. It contained our code of

ethics, our sense of self and duty. It also contained all our stories.

The upside of the King keeping the Book under lock and key, is our stories were safe.

Downside? If someone did get to the Book, they wouldn't need the King's approval to rewrite it. Legend said if someone had the Bone Flute, they could rewrite any rhyme, story, or tale they wanted to.

You'd think we'd have the Bone Flute locked up and secure, but no. It had been lost years ago, buried in an unmarked grave in the Tulgey Wood.

I'd never heard of the gang, the Sins before, but no person or creature could live in Las Fables without a rhyme or a story to hold them here.

"Why do they want a woman to deliver the Book?" Horner asked.

"Maybe because we're such harmless dolls?" Muffet's smile would make anyone think twice about that.

"Muffet, get out to the scene and keep tempers calm," I said. "Horner, get the Book and meet us out there as soon as you can."

"I'll need King Cole's permission and the key to Goose's Vault," Horner said. "Peter, you know the King. Trying to talk him into that could take days."

"We don't have days. You've got a finger in a lot of pies. Tell King Cole it's life or death. Snow's life or death."

I hoped the King cared more about his daughter-in-law than his control over the Book.

"What are you going to do?" Muffet asked.

"Save Snow White."

I'd never expected to put on a corset and tights in the name of duty, but if keeping my city safe meant wearing a bra, then sign me up for a double-D.

I rubbed a palm over my rib cage checking for the pistol under the lace and frills. Hostage situations could get ugly fast, and I wasn't about to be caught with my bloomers down.

"How many Sins are in there?" I asked Horner as I adjusted my wig. We were in the little glen just outside the Seven Dwarves' cottage, a creek rippling nearby.

The whole force had turned out to make sure this went as smooth as my currently shaved legs.

"We counted seven," Horner said.

"Names?"

"Angry, Greedy, Lusty, Envy, Lazy, Gluttony, and Cocky."

"Who's the leader?"

"Cocky."

Of course. "What do we have on them?"

Horner pulled out a rap sheet as long as his arm.

"Angry: fourteen counts assault. Greedy: nine counts embezzlement. Lusty: six counts of indecent exposure. Envy: three counts car keying. Gluttony: multiple counts dine and dash. Lazy's a litterbug, and Cocky's been busted for one thing: using magic beans to buy a cow from an impoverished youth."

Muffet strolled over from where she'd been keeping watch on the Dwarves' cottage with the other officers.

"Just got news the King is in his counting house, counting out ransom money if we need it.' She gave me a wide smile. "You look good in lace, Boss."

"I would have gone with something in a jewel tone though," Horner said. "Better with your complexion."

"Oh, yeah," Muffet said. "Jewel tone would be nice."

"Save it," I said, as sternly as I could with satin panties riding up my rear. "Horner, you're on the horn. Offer money first."

Horner knew the spiel, but I had to get my mind off the smolder in Muffet's gaze.

"You know what a good boy am I," Horner said. "Luck, Peter." He clapped me on the shoulder and strode over to the line of cars facing the cottage.

"I should be the one going in there, Boss," Muffet said.

She was right. The Sins had demanded a woman deliver the Book. Muffet was the best woman on the force right now. But if a bug got in her line of vision, the entire cottage and everyone in it could go up in smoke.

"I need you out here for backup."

"You're afraid I'll torch the place."

"It's not that I don't trust you."

"I've done the counseling," she reminded me, her chin tipped up. "Got all the gold stars."

"I know."

"I can handle pressure. No matter how buggy it gets. So why not send me in?"

"Seven criminals," I said. "Seven stories that aren't in the Book. If anyone's going to gamble their life on those odds, it's gonna be me."

She was silent for a few beats. "You know you don't have to save all of Las Fables on your own, Peter," she said quietly.

Hearing her use my first name kicked me in the heart. "I never told you I was trying to."

She gave me a bemused look. "No," she said, "you didn't."

We stood there a moment, caught in the possibility of saying something, doing something that could change what we were to each other. Something that might change our stories and our lives.

Her focus was so intense, I felt like I'd been lost in the woods, and she was the church bell calling me home.

Then the moment drifted away, and she tapped the edge of her beret in a jaunty salute.

"Be careful, Boss. Remember we've got your back. Well," she said with a grin, "your bustle."

Horner waved her over, and she jogged off, leaving nothing but the sweet scent of bug spray behind.

CHAPTER 9

I tugged at the corset, adjusting the revolver against my ribs. I only had six shots if it came down to dirt. Six shots for seven Sins.

I bent and adjusted my garter, checking the book bound in red leather strapped against my thigh. It wasn't *the* Book, but it was the closest replica Horner could find.

King Cole had refused to give Horner the key to the Goose's Vault that held the Book. The Queen of Hearts had argued letting Horner have it would save Snow White's life.

The Queen's sudden support of Snow surprised me. I didn't think the royal mother cared much for her daughter-in-law.

But the King proved he cared even less and had ignored both the Queen and Horner's pleas. The

Queen had been furious, but there was nothing she could do to change Cole's mind.

The replica book was a quality reproduction, with LAS FABLES embossed in fancy gold script across the cover. But one look inside at the cheap paper and common inks gave it away as a fake.

If things went sideways, and I had to hard over the replica, the jig would be up.

I fluffed my skirt, took a couple practice steps in the heels, and tried not to break an ankle.

"Cocky," Horner's voice boomed through the bullhorn. "We need to talk."

Show time.

"No negotiations," a voice answered from the cottage. "The Book."

"We are willing to offer money," Horner said.

There was a pause, a silence in the forest. I thought I heard an argument in the cottage, then Cocky was back.

"No money—"

"How much money?" a second voice called out.

"No money!" Cocky shouted. "If we don't get the Book by midnight, your little Princess is dead."

Then I smelled it—the delicious fragrance of apple pie wafting through the air.

I didn't know how those dirty thugs had pulled it off. Apples had been outlawed ever since Snow White had gotten a bite of that killer Granny Smith.

Horner switched tactics immediately.

"Fine, no money. You send out Snow White, unharmed, and we'll send in the Book."

"I'm not stupid, Copper! Send the Book to us first, then you'll get the Princess."

"Halfway," Horner suggested. "Snow White and the Book are exchanged at the door."

Cocky thought that one over. I took a deep breath and nearly passed out. Next time I wore drag, I'd loosen the corset.

"That was my idea, Cop," Cocky called back. "Send in your girl with the Book, and we'll give you Snow White at the door. Those are my rules, my idea, my final offer."

Horner nodded at me, and I trotted down the path. "We're sending the girl and the Book now."

"Make her undress," a different voice yelled.

I stopped dead in my tracks. This could be a problem.

I glanced at Horner. The flicker of surprise was wiped away by a frown as he shuffled tactics.

Muffet just grinned like a Cheshire at a tea party and gave me a huge wink.

I couldn't help but smile back at her. She flashed a cheesy thumbs up, and mouthed: *You got this, girl.*

I wondered how long it would take to kiss that smile off her face.

"That's not going to happen, Cocky," Horner said. "The girl stays clothed."

Muffet fake-frowned and mouthed: *Boo*.

"Fine," Cocky said. "Just bring the Book."

Good ol' Horner could pull a plum out of any situation.

I turned, tossed golden tresses over my shoulder, and pursed my lips. I strutted down the path to the cottage door and knocked.

The lock slid. The door pulled back.

A little creature the size and shape of a dwarf stood in the doorway. Instead of rosy cheeks and colorful clothes, he wore a black leather jacket and pants with enough studs, chains, and rivets, he could bolt Humpty Dumpty together again.

"What the hell?" the little guy said.

He had to be the one called Angry.

"I have the Book," I said in the most virginal falsetto I could muster.

He grabbed me with his huge mitts and yanked me into the house. I tripped over my heels but caught myself as he slammed the door.

So much for the tradeoff at the door.

Sins lined the room—a couple by the window, one sitting in the corner, and all of them staring at me. I decided it was best to play dumb until I knew who was who.

"Oh!" I squealed. "Why you're not children at all. You're little men."

"Stand there and shut up, girly," Angry growled.

"I wanted to say that!" Envy stomped his foot.

"Well, well," Lusty leered, licking his lips.

"And so big," Greedy said.

The one standing in a pile of brown pastry boxes and downing an entire cherry tart must be Gluttony.

The little guy in the corner snoring it up had to be Lazy, which meant the slick-haired joker in the pin-striped suit in front of me was Cocky.

"My plan was perfect!" Cocky crowed. "I told you I could lure them in. I told you they'd bow to my demands. I told you—"

"—you told us we'd get a vacation," Angry growled. "How hard can it be to get one book without bringing out the entire police force?" He waved at the window where lights flashed red and blue.

"I—" Envy began.

Angry bulldozed over him. "We should have stayed home."

"I wanted to say that!" Envy said.

"More money there," Greedy agreed. "More wine, more women, more song, more..."

"...women, definitely," Lusty murmured.

"You have a woman," Cocky said. "A hostage—which was my idea. You'll get your vacation once my plan is complete."

"What plan?" I asked.

Cocky eyed me. "Tell me your name, toots."

"Miss Muffet."

"So, it goes like this, Muffet." He put one manicured finger on his lips.

"Little Miss Muffet lay on her tuffet ..."

"Kissing both Curtis and Wayne," Lusty added.

"The bank man, he spied her..." Greedy said.

"Took both of her lovers..." Gluttony said.

"And Muffet blew all three away!" Angry yelled.

Not only would that rewrite turn Muffet into a murderer instead of an arachnophobe, the damn thing didn't rhyme very well.

"That's terrible!"

"Of course it is," Cocky said. "When we get done rewriting the rhymes of Las Fables, I'll be famous!"

"And rich!" Greedy said.

"And tall!" Envy added.

Lusty had a look in his eyes that told me exactly what he wanted out of all this.

I had to get Snow White out of here, pronto.

"Where's the other girl?" I asked, batting my eyes.

"What other girl?" Cocky asked.

"Snow White." Nothing. "The hostage you're trading for the Book?"

The seven little Sins looked at each other and shuffled their feet. Something wasn't right.

"Yeah." Cocky snapped his fingers. "She's tied up in the kitchen."

"Gagged," Angry added a little too quickly.

"And, uh, unconscious," Lusty said.

My gut twisted like a dish of half-baked blackbirds. They were lying.

Cocky's eyes did double-time trying to watch both me and the kitchen door. So, I headed to the door.

"What did you do to her?" I asked.

"You can't go in there!" Cocky squeaked.

Gluttony set his feet and squared his sizable bulk in front of the door.

I was about to find out what kind of ramming speed I could build up in heels when the kitchen door swung open and whacked Gluttony so hard, he fish-flopped onto the freshly swept stone floor.

There, in the doorway to the kitchen, stood Snow White. Raven hair spilled down her narrow shoulders, her pale face gone ghostly white.

She wore a frilly apron over her black judge's robe and didn't seem to be harmed. But my heart hit my loafers when I saw the apple pies in her hands.

Juice dripped unnoticed down her arms and cinnamon dusted her red lips. Snow White had been tasting the forbidden fruit.

All those years in Apple Eaters Anonymous, washed down the drain.

"Oh, dear," Snow said to Gluttony. "I should have

called out before coming through, but to be fair, you shouldn't have been standing so close to the door in the first place."

Gluttony, unconscious, didn't reply.

"I rule we should both be more careful next time," she said. "Now we'll forget this little mishap and carry on. No fines. Dismissed."

The Fairest in the Land smiled a crooked, sunny smile. "Now my seven little men, who wants more pie?"

She looked around the room.

Spotted me.

"Peter?"

CHAPTER 10

Snow looked me up from white hose to padded bosom, confusion, recognition, and guilt doing the 23-skidoo across her face.

"Snow," I said, all pretense of femininity forgotten, "it's time to leave."

She stepped toward me, weaving. "I suspected you'd be along to visit me and my little seven, Peter. But I didn't think you'd dress up for the occasion. Is that a new uniform, Detective?"

"Detective?" Cocky said.

"Peter?" Lusty demanded.

"You said you were a dame," Angry growled.

Snow White giggled, a desperate sound bubbling up from under a mountain of grief.

The Dwarves' death had hit her harder than I'd expected.

"Oh, you all know Peter. Right, Peter?" she said. "And you remember the Seven Dwarves, don't you? See? They're alive. Still alive. All of them. All seven.

"Nothing bad happened. Nothing bad happened at all. I'm going to stay with them and make pies and everything will be fine again. Everyone will be happy."

"Snow," I said gently. "Taking care of a bunch of lowlife Sins isn't going to bring the Dwarves back. The Seven are gone for good. Just put the pies down, and I'll take you home."

"Home?"

"The Charming castle."

She licked cinnamon off the corner of her lips. "You must be mistaken. I am home. We're all fine here. Happy here."

"Time to go to your *real* home," I said.

"No one's going anywhere." Cocky moved in on me, Greedy at his back. "Give me the Book."

"Not a chance," I pulled handcuffs out of my brassiere. "I'm Detective Peter Peter, and you are all under arrest."

Lusty licked his lips and smiled. "Ooh, bondage."

"I don't think so, Copper," Cocky said.

"Seven of us and only one of you," Greedy said.

"We'll just kill you, then take the Book!" Angry bellowed.

The Sins drew together like a pack of vicious dogs.

Even Lazy and Gluttony picked themselves up for the fight.

All of them had some sort of blunt weapon in their hand: a rolling pin, a club, a chair leg, a bowling ball.

I was fumbling with the laces of my corset, struggling to get at my gun.

"Down!" I yelled at Snow, who ducked and covered behind the kitchen door.

"Freeze!" I warned the Sins.

They lunged.

Envy took a bullet to the chest. "First!" he gasped before he crumpled.

Lusty jumped on me and ripped off one of my fake bosoms. I clobbered him on the back of the head. He dropped to the floor and lay still.

The rest was a blur. Angry chewed my ankle, Gluttony banged a pie pan into my stomach, and Lazy, well, he really didn't do much more than die in his sleep. Greedy picked through the pockets of his fallen comrades until a bullet hit his shriveled heart.

Then there were only two left standing—Cocky and me.

"Pumpkin eater," he sneered, "you aren't worth the words that wrote you." He adjusted his grip on the pickax over his shoulder.

I leveled the gun at his greasy little head. "Put the ax down, Cocky. You and your gang are done. You'll never be a story in this town."

"Not without the Book." Cocky twisted, but instead of swinging the ax, he threw an apple at my head.

I sidestepped.

One of my stilettos caught in a cobble and snapped like a stick in the mud. I wobbled like a chopped bean stalk.

Cocky was fast but his apple aim was terrible. His aim when he swung the ax wasn't so good either.

The blade swiped the back of my hand and sent my gun skidding across the floor.

My garter slipped and something thumped between my feet.

The Book.

Cocky jumped for it, but I was quick. I scooped it up and threw the Book at him.

I've been a cop for a long time. When I throw the Book at someone, they go down for years.

The Book hit him right between the eyes and knocked him out cold.

My heart hammered like a shoe shop of full of elves working a rush order.

The Sins began to fade.

There was no rhyme, no story, no ink to hold them to this city. They melted like watered witches, fading back to wherever they had come from.

In moments, there was nothing left of the Sins but white chalk outlines.

"Judge White? Snow?" I called out. "Are you okay?"

"No." She stepped out from behind the kitchen door. "I'm not okay. You killed them." A tear slid down her pale cheek.

"They're dead again. This isn't fair, Peter. I don't want—nothing is the same. Is this my life now? This? How is this right?"

I didn't know how to answer that. The Seven shouldn't be dead. The Sins shouldn't have tried to take their place.

Losing the Dwarves was already making Las Fables unstable. Already affecting our stories.

Already affecting her.

The door burst open and Muffet strode in, a spray can in each hand and a fierce look in her eyes.

Horner was right behind her.

"Clear?" Muffet asked.

"Clear," I said. "Muffet, please help Judge White."

Muffet stowed her cans and stepped over to Snow.

Horner holstered his gun and pulled out his notebook, already jotting details of the scene.

I retrieved the fake Book from where it lay in the dust.

"Okay, Boss?" Horner asked.

"For now," I said.

"Ma'am?" Muffet said. "Let's get you some fresh air. Can you walk with me, Judge White?"

Snow brushed her fingers over her cheeks and sniffed. She straightened her apron and hair.

"Of course I can walk. Everything is under control. I knew the force would be here to take care of the Sev—Sins."

"Yes, Ma'am," Muffet said.

Snow strode crisply toward me. "A commendable job, Detective Peter. You have our royal thanks for your speedy intervention. That isn't the actual Book, is it?"

"No Ma'am. The King didn't want to risk it falling into the wrong hands."

Her lips twisted like she'd just bit a bit of bitter butter. "Of course. Can't risk his power just to save a life, can we?"

I opened my mouth to answer, but she was already moving.

"Let's have that fresh air," she said to Muffet.

"This way, Your Honor." Muffet placed her hand on Snow's elbow and walked her out the door.

Horner pointed at the chalk outlines. "Is that all that's left of the Sins?"

"Yes."

"What happened?"

"Once I figure that out, you can read it in my report."

I handed him the book. "Take this back to the King, would you?"

He tucked it beneath his overcoat. "You sure you're okay, Boss?"

It was a good question. But I didn't have a good answer.

"If you want to talk about it…" He clapped me on the shoulder, waited a second, then left.

I pulled off the wig, the morning breeze cooling the sweat on my face and neck.

Something had happened here. Something more than seven Sins trying to shoehorn their way into town.

Something more than a grieving woman desperately seeking something she lost.

There was a story here, written between the lines in a way I couldn't quite get a read on.

The King was involved. Withholding the real Book, arguing with the Queen, taking chances with other people's lives, and not wanting to risk his power, according to Snow.

She was involved too, wishing for a home that was no longer real, a life she could no longer have, her story as it had been written forever changed.

Endings happened. Not all of them were happily ever after.

A skittering at the kitchen door made me spin.

"Smile, Peter!" Chic Ken Little thumbed his camera. The room flashed white.

"Beea-utiful!" he hooted. "Today's paper was good, but you're gonna love tomorrow's headline."

"This is a crime scene, Chic. Get out of here."

"Freedom of press."

"Contamination of a crime scene. Exit the cottage."

"Ooh. I'm scared." He lifted the camera.

Tom Stout strolled in and assessed the situation. "We need your statement, Boss. Want me to deal with Mr. Little?"

"Yes. Escort him off the premises immediately."

Tom stepped aside and waved at the open door. "You heard the man."

Chic snapped a couple more photos.

"Now, Mr. Little." Stout took a step toward him.

"I'm going, I'm going." Chic strolled out, whistling about mulberry bushes and popped weasels.

"Anything else, Boss?" Tom asked.

"Take this into evidence." I handed him my gun. He slid it into a bag.

"If you need me," I said, "I'll be at the station filling out paperwork."

The report was a strange thing to read, even for me, the reporting officer.

The facts were easy to recount, even if the gut

feeling that I'd seen more than I could explain lingered.

Horner knocked on my office doorway. "Snow's doing better."

"And Chuck Charming?"

"He'll be in later. He sounded concerned and consoling. I think Snow might finally be coming to terms with the Dwarves' death."

I grunted. Maybe. But the grief I'd seen in her was real and deep. It was going to take more than a day to erase.

Horner sat in the chair on the other side of my desk and rocked it back on two legs.

"You did a good job out there, Peter. Two tough cases in two days. What are the odds?"

"Against the house. Something's wrong, Horner. Las Fables is changing."

He shrugged. "Las Fables never changes. It's just life in the big city."

"Or it's something else."

My gut said these were big changes. Dark changes slipping through the night like the shadow I'd almost seen, the whiffling I'd barely heard.

Horner nodded toward the report on my desk. "You want to talk about it now?"

"You mean how I handled the situation no better than a prince looking for a liplock to fame? Or how I paraded around in front of the entire police force in a pink evening gown and stiletto heels?"

"Are you angry about the dress?"

"Not the dress. The guy in it."

"What about the guy in it?"

"He's missing something. Something just out of sight."

Horner frowned. "A clue?"

"No. Well, maybe, but no."

"You want to interview the Old Woman again? Or Snow? We could ask around. See if anyone saw the Sins make their move to enter Las Fables."

I rubbed the back of my neck. If I didn't have words for it, there wouldn't be a way to make Horner understand. "It's been a long day. I'm beat."

"You sure you don't want me to set up interviews?"

"No need."

Horner eased out of the chair and gathered the remains of the dress I'd left in the corner.

"You did the right thing taking on the Sins," he said. "Snow wasn't thinking clearly. Those Sins were out to destroy everyone's stories. You kept Snow and Las Fables safe.

"Story and duty, Peter. That's what the guy in the dress did today."

"Yeah," I said. "Story and duty."

He stepped toward the door.

"Horner?"

He glanced back.

"Leave the panties."

He gave me a long look, the corner of his mouth twitching up, flat lining, then curving up again.

He sorted the satin panties out of the folds of fabric and dangled them a minute before dropping them on my desk.

He had a million questions in his eyes, and not a single word on his lips.

Like I said, he was the best partner a man could have.

"Good-bye, Horner." I turned back to the paperwork.

"See ya, Boss." He grinned then headed off.

CHAPTER 11

I'd tried to catch some shuteye in my office after Horner left, but sleep wouldn't keep me.

Just before dawn, I wandered outside to smoke and watch the sky for falling cows.

The man in the moon looked down on a street as empty as a genie's fourth wish. I didn't know what was on the moon's mind, but I was thinking about dwarves, death, and dames.

Dwarves and death I could handle. But dames were another story.

I still couldn't shake the feeling that I'd let Snow down with the whole Sin situation, even though I'd followed story and duty to the letter.

The fact was, I had as much luck with women as Humpty Dumpty had walking a high wire.

In my line of work it was easy to fall for the first teary-eyed puss in boots that came along.

But finding someone to spend a life with, finding someone to love, wasn't easy-peasy.

I inhaled smoke, exhaled slowly.

Memories of my ex-wife, Peggy, always came with regret. Our stories were doomed to play out the way they had—her breaking the law, me locking her away.

All for story and duty.

She'd pleaded innocent, of course. Said Humpty had jumped.

But everyone knows eggs don't do the big over easy on their own.

Judge White had given her twenty years.

When women were good, they were very, very good, and when they were bad, well, they were very, very good at that too.

Still, there was one gal I couldn't get out of my mind: Muffet.

The glimmer of humor in her eyes when she thought I was being stubborn, her steady confidence in the face of danger, her soft laughter drifting across the station making grim days brighter.

She'd been giving me looks lately. Looks I'd seen Horner give Blue. I wasn't sure how I should respond to that.

Didn't know how she wanted me to.

But I knew I wanted more out of life than a hard job and an empty bottle at the end of the day.

Still, making a move like Paddy had suggested, and actually dating Muffet?

My story didn't end in a happily ever after. What kind of a man would drag a peach like Muffet into a rotten rhyme like mine?

Movement shifted in the alley across the street.

I squinted but a heifer hit optimal orbit and crossed the face of the moon. Cow shadow hid the figures on the street and blacked out the night. When old Bessie's orbit deteriorated, the shadows were gone.

Somewhere in the distance, a little dog laughed.

The town clock struck five bells and the wind rose. I found myself holding my breath. Waiting. Waiting to hear a sound that shouldn't exist in Las Fables—a whiffle.

But other than the clatter of running cutlery, all was quiet.

I exhaled on a chuckle. I was worked up for nothing. As jumpy as a froggy gone a courting.

I flicked the cigarette to the ground, scraped it out with my shoe, then made my way back into the station.

Horner was already in his corner taking notes from Chuck Charming who wore a magnificent purple cape gilded with gold.

I grunted, having not expected the royal to come in this early of his own volition.

I figured Horner was getting an earful of what the TDH thought about the Sins, and why he had been at the bar the night of the Dwarves' murder.

The Old Woman had already confessed to the crime, so his statement wasn't required.

But the Prince was the sort of character who dotted his i's and crossed everyone's t's whether they liked it or not.

"Ah! Detective Peter." His smile was stiff as a twenty dollar shot. He motioned me to join him and Horner.

I stopped by Jack's desk. "Your Highness."

"I was just giving my recollection of the other night in the bar. Ghastly business."

"Terrible," Horner agreed with an ace-in-the-hole poker face. He didn't point out the fake sympathy of Chuck's tone. He didn't have to.

"Have you recalled anyone who might have wanted the Dwarves dead?" I asked. "Anyone who may have brought a complaint to you?"

Chuck leaned back, thoughtful as a ten-o'clock scholar. "It could be the Sins."

We knew it wasn't. They hadn't arrived in town until after the Dwarves were dead.

"Anyone else?" I pressed.

"There have been...discussions of where the boundary of the Tulgey Wood begins and ends."

"Discussions?" I wondered where he was going with this.

He flicked his hand as if batting away a fly. "It's a very old, long-simmering dispute. The Three Pigs have forwarded yet another complaint that the land on the other side of the Dwarves' property line—where the river runs through the Tulgey Wood—actually belongs to the Pigs."

Horner rubbed a finger between his eyebrows. "They've been fighting over that for years, haven't they?"

Chuck pointed in agreement. "Which is why it didn't occur to me to bring it up. Their complaint isn't new, nor was the outcome of Snow siding once again with the Dwarves and ruling that the property line remains as it is."

"You think the Pigs finally snapped and killed the Seven over a bit of river?" Horner asked.

"I will leave that to the experts. What I do know is that Snow has changed her mind. The property line will be redrawn. The Pigs will finally own a section of the river and can do with it as they please."

I weighed that new bit of information. "When did Snow White give her ruling?"

"Late last night. After being held by the Sins in the Dwarves' cottage. She wants nothing of that wretched place now and would rather the Pigs tear it down and build over it."

He looked pleased as a puss in a canary cage that she'd finally turned her back on the Seven.

"Is there anything else you can think of?" I asked.

His smile flattened. "Yes. Something else came to me last night. I've heard a strange sound."

"What kind of sound?" I asked.

His dark brows dipped. "It's difficult to describe."

"Do you think it's threatening?"

"It could be? Perhaps it could be."

"Why haven't you mentioned it before?" Horner asked.

"It's not the sort of thing someone like me—a man true to his story—should admit, I suppose." He glanced at his nails. "These things are below me. Monsters and Nary Tales."

We waited while he dilly-dallied.

"It was a…a whiffle." He cleared his throat, nervous as Cock Robin at an archery tournament. "I know it's ridiculous. Nothing whiffles in Las Fables."

He was right. Nothing should whiffle here. There was no story for that kind of sound.

"All right," Horner said, gamely. "Things have been stressful lately, what with the murder, the Sins. Maybe you just need a little rest…"

"I believe you," I cut in.

Horner blinked, then slowly shook his head, watching for the lie he would not find on my face.

"As you should," Chuck said, "I'm telling the truth, as unlikely as it sounds. I've consulted the histories, the Unwritten, the Nary Tales. I am convinced there is a great beast set loose upon our land."

"A dragon?" Horner asked.

"Something darker, even more fierce. If I am right, if my research is correct..." He paused for dramatic effect, because why wouldn't he, "...it is a Jabberwock."

My brain blank-paged. Nary Tales were stories made up to frighten little children. Believing a monster out of a Nary Tale was real and here in Las Fables was ludicrous.

Still, I'd heard something too, hadn't I? An uncommon sound. Something that could have been the fabled whiffle of the Jabberwock on the hunt.

Any common citizen would be called a fool for believing in the monster.

But Chuck Charming was not a common citizen. The royals were written in uppercase above all us lowercase chumps. If Chuck wanted to believe in a Nary Tale, no one would challenge him.

"Do you want us to send out a search party?" I asked.

Horner made a small sound of disbelief but turned his attention back to his notes.

"That won't be necessary," the Prince said, haughtily. "I intend to hunt it myself."

"The Jabberwock," I repeated, just to make sure he heard the words coming out of his mouth.

"Yes."

"Let's say you hunt it. Let's say you find a monster," I said. "Do you have a, uh...vorpal sword to snicker-snack?"

His lip curled. "You dare mock me?"

"Just the facts, Your Highness. Do you have the correct weapons? Do you want back up? Guards? Members of the force?"

"I need no one." He stood and glowered at me. "I am perfectly capable of hunting beasts on my own. I am a Charming, after all, and have defeated evil witches, giants, and dragons alike."

I expected him to exit stage left after that grand proclamation, but he had one more shoe to drop. "Also, there is to be a royal ball to celebrate Snow's and my royal wedding anniversary. My mother, the Queen, requests your presence to discuss security. You will attend her."

"Trouble with the witches?" Horner asked.

"Not as yet," he said. "But one must stay ever vigilant." He cleared his throat and raised his voice. "Now I must leave. There is a beast to hunt and a kingdom to protect."

Every person in the joint stopped and stared at him, transfixed.

He raised his chin and pointed into the distance as if the pathway of his quest rolled out ahead of him, beckoning.

"Fear not, small citizens of the land. For I shall protect you!" He strode through the station, regal, proud, and terribly unforgettable.

A few people bowed as he passed, some clapped politely, one threw a couple cockleshells at his feet.

Chuck paused at the door. He swished that magnificent kingly cape, then strode onward and outward, the hero, the prince, the superstory.

People started chattering again, someone cussed, someone laughed, and the station was back to normal.

Horner blew out a breath. "That was something."

"You got it all written down?"

"You know I do. I'll bring the notes once I get them organized. Food in the back, if you want breakfast." His phone rang and he picked it up.

I was hungry, so I stopped at a table where a few late-night leftovers were left over and a few new snacks were stacked.

A peck of peppers was the primary pick. I plucked a portion of the pickled produce, promptly pocketed my peckish preference, pivoted and proceeded to pace placidly toward my professional post.

The station door opened, and wind whooshed into the room.

I turned, expecting Chuck Charming to have returned for another dramatic announcement.

Standing just inside the room, hanging her coat on the hook so her back was toward me, was the most gorgeous woman I'd ever laid eyes on. My gaze lingered over the curve of her calves, her tight tuffet, and the unbound silk of yellow hair curtaining the peekaboo show of bare shoulders.

Her dress was red as Snow's lips and tight as a witch's britches.

She turned.

My peck fell out of my pocket.

It was Muffet.

CHAPTER 12

Gone were the black pants and jacket Muffet usually wore. Gone were the bug traps and cans of bug spray holstered at each hip.

Muffet was one hundred percent dreamy dame in a ruby red slip of a dress that would make any Jack fall on his knees and beg to tumble down her hill.

She caught me looking and sauntered my way.

Each step gave me a glimpse of the lacy black garter riding the curve of her thigh.

I'd never wanted to be a garter so badly in my life.

"Morning, Boss," she said, eyeing me from shoe to shave. "You're up early."

I had to swallow to find my voice. "You're up late."

She narrowed her eyes at my own rumpled appearance. "Looks like we both had a long, hot night." Then she added, "At least one of us had fun."

"You're out of uniform," I croaked.

"Got a change of clothes in my locker."

Her gaze, which was deeper and greener than I'd ever seen, stirred me down to my penal codes. "Thanks for noticing."

I caught a whiff of her perfume, cinnamon and sugar, sweet and spicy, as she sashayed by.

Horner nodded at her as she passed, then made his way to where I was still standing and staring.

"Feeling okay, Peter? You're sweating."

"It's hot in here," I muttered as I adjusted my produce, tucking it back into my pocket.

Horner followed my gaze to Muffet. "She's out of uniform."

"I see that."

"That's quite a dress she has on." His eyes cut to me, full of merriment. "Don't you think? Quite a dress. Fits her like a wolf in sheep's clothing. Like she was sewn into every inch of it."

I tore my gaze away from Muffet so I could scowl at my partner instead.

"You know, now that I think of it," Horner said with a grin, "it *is* hot in here. Red hot, no, *cinnamon* hot."

"Breeze off, you big bazoo." I strode to my office, but he dogged my heels.

He chuckled and dropped into the chair on the other side of my desk. "Ask her out."

I hung my coat on the hook. "Dangle, Jack."

"I think she's waiting for you to make the first move."

"Work to do," I said. "Cases to solve. Murders. Are there any new leads from the Shoe Bar?"

"No." He rubbed fingers over his mouth and leaned back, making the chair creak. "There hasn't been any new information at all."

"The Bears?"

"Didn't find a single out-of-place fingerprint."

"Bullets?"

"Matched the Old Woman's gun. It looks like she did it."

I grunted. Looks could be deceiving, especially in Las Fables.

"What's your take on the Prince?" I asked.

"The Nary Tale a-hunting he will go? It's not one for the money, but it's two for the show, that's for sure. Typical dramatic TDH."

"True."

"What I want to know is why you sided with him."

"How so?"

"You really believe he heard a whiffle? In Las Fables?"

"Maybe I was just doing my job. Listening, learning, getting him to talk."

Horner snicked air through his teeth. "No, you believed him. Why?"

"Maybe I've been hearing strange things in Las Fables lately, too."

"A whiffle?" At my silence, his eyes widened. "You think you heard a Nary Tale? C'mon, Peter."

"Two disasters in two days," I countered, "and now the Prince has gone heigh-ho the derry-oh for a monster. Something is happening between the lines. Something we can't see."

"All right," he allowed. "But you aren't the kind of guy who believes in nonsense."

"No. But I am the kind of guy who trusts my gut. Something hinky's going on."

"Do you want me to follow the Prince?"

Not a bad suggestion, but chances were the Prince would be back by cowfall tonight. "We don't need to follow him, we're already one step behind. We need to get ahead of this."

"How do you get ahead of something we haven't figured out, or in the case of the Prince's monster, might not even exist?"

"We bring in the psychics."

Horner looked at me like I'd gone Simon in the head. "Are you sure?"

Neither of us believed in mumbo-jumbo hocus-pocus stuff. To detectives like Horner and me, psychics were as unbelievable as the existence of Jabberwocks, Bandersnatches, and fair taxation.

But the psychics had led us straight on other cases,

including the lost kitten mitten mystery and finding where oh where that little dog had gone. It was worth giving them a shot now.

"I'm sure. Call them in."

"Will do, Boss." He rapped knuckles on my desk, stood, and walked out.

I lit a cigarette and took a few drags.

The last two days were a puzzle of missing pieces. Seven Dwarves fighting. The Old Woman blowing them away. Sins demanding the Book. The Prince chasing imaginary monsters.

Except I'd heard the whiffle too, hadn't I?

Maybe the stress of the job—story and duty—was finally getting to me.

In next to no time, Horner was back. "The psychics," he announced.

Three Blind Mice wearing dark glasses and carrying white canes pattered into my office.

The tan mouse, Hickory, skittered up to the top of my desk and announced: "It's the Farmer's Wife!"

"Yes!" agreed the brown mouse, Dickory. "Lock her up. Lock up the Farmer's Wife!"

Ever since the Farmer's Wife had gotten liquored up and pulled that Ginsu-roulette stunt, the Mice had turned rat-fink. Now whenever a crime came up, the Mice found a way to accuse her of it.

"You're saying the Farmer's Wife cut a deal with a Nary Tale monster?" I asked.

"She cuts tails," Hickory said.

"She cuts everything," Dickory added.

The gray mouse muttered something under his breath, then hauled himself up onto the top of my desk next to the others. "Wasn't the Wife," he said.

"Don't listen to Dock, Detective," Hickory said. "Ever since the clock struck him, he hasn't been the same."

Dickory made circular motions with his finger by his ear.

"We need information on a monster," I said. "Here in Las Fables. Have you heard a whiffle?"

The Blind Mice all went still except for their trembling whiskers.

Finally, Dock spoke. "I heard..."

"He heard the Wife!" Hickory interrupted.

"I heard..."

"...the sound of the carving knife!" Dickory tried to clap a hand over Dock's mouth but missed.

"I heard talking," Dock said. "A woman talking about keys and sweets and pipes—no, flutes."

Those were all stock story things to speak about, but Dock had good ears. There must have been something strange about the conversation to make him remember.

"Anything else?" I asked.

"I thought I heard a whiffle," Dock said.

Horner and I exchanged a look.

"Who was the woman talking?" Horner asked.

"The Wife. It was probably the Wife," Hickory said.

Horner's expression let me know just how reliable he thought the Mice really were, but I wasn't ready to give up on a lead—any lead.

"Would you recognize her voice if you heard her again?" I asked Dock.

"Sure," he said.

"Where did you hear the conversation?" Horner asked.

"In the Tulgey Wood," Dock said. "Cut by the Seven Dwarves' place."

CHAPTER 13

There we had it. Another clue leading us back to the Dwarves.

"Hickory, Dickory," I said. "Thank you for your time. Dock, I want you to go out to the Dwarves' place and around town with Officer Horner here. See if you can pick up the woman's voice."

"Happy to help," Dock said.

"Drop a dime," I told Horner.

"Will do, Boss." Horner lowered his hand to the Mice, and they all clambered aboard.

I put on my hat and coat and made my way to Muffet's desk. She sat on her tuffet, flipping through a book of arachnid mugshots.

She'd changed out of the dress. Back in her usual black shirt, trousers and boots, she could kick a crooked man straight.

I noticed a flyer tucked under a stack of paper-work. It said there was a new torch singer in town. Said the name of the act was Sugar and Spice. Below that, was a picture of Muffet in a slinky red slip.

"Come with me," I said.

"Sure, Boss." She snapped the book shut, and settled her red beret at an angle on her head. "Where to?"

"The Royal Castle."

"Is this about the ball?"

We strode toward the door. "How'd you hear?"

She grabbed a Sixpence Slinger off a desk as we passed and handed it to me, never breaking stride. "Front page."

The announcement of the Charmings' ball and anniversary made a splash above and below the fold. There would be dancing, drinks, entertainment. At midnight they'd put on a full reenactment of Snow White's original rescue from the evil queen.

"Open to the public," Muffet pointed out.

"I see that."

"I do love to dance," she said.

I grunted and held the door open for her before following her into the sunlight. "Hope you can do it in your boots. You'll be on security duty."

"Oh, I can do all sorts of things in my boots, Boss." She tossed me a smile with a spin-the-bottle dare in her eyes.

I pushed down a grin.

The day had gone shiny, sunlight like warm honey pouring over the town.

Plenty of regular folk were on the street: near-sighted Lucy Locket looking for her pocket, while Penny Fisher waved it in front of her face.

A couple frogs with paper crowns tipped jauntily on their heads hopped toward the nearest pond for their eight-to-five kiss-me-I'm-a-prince gig, and a donkey, dog, cat, and rooster argued over the words to a song.

Innocent people following story and duty. Not a one of them would believe in Nary Tales.

"Page two," Muffet said as we crossed past the Muffin Man's shop and through the community garden blooming with silver bells and maids all in a row.

I turned to page two. The headline announced: MALLBERRY'S GRAND OPENING. Beneath that was a picture of the Three Pigs in tailored vests. They stood in front of a large fountain I'd never seen before.

"Where's this?" I folded the paper to read the article.

"Out in the Tulgey Wood. The Pigs didn't waste any time with Snow's ruling."

"By the Dwarves' place?"

"Not far."

"Those Pigs know how to build fast."

"Sure, but not everything they build holds up. I like slow and steady, you know? Building up things slow, so they last."

I tugged at my collar and tried to think of something pithy to say when she reached into her back pocket and pulled out a piece of paper. "You need to see this."

I tucked the Slinger under my arm and unfolded the flyer. "Witches are done with the bubble and are boiling up trouble? How is that news?"

"Look where they're gathering."

I tipped the flyer.

"Tulgey Wood. Mallberry's. Today."

She nodded. "They've never liked the Pigs. Hate that they built in the Wood. Figure they'll protest peaceful like?"

Witches, like fairies, were tricky when they didn't get their way. Take for example the Thirteenth, who got all bent out of shape when she didn't get invited to a baby shower.

"One more thing to keep an eye on." I handed her the flyer, which she pocketed. "First, let's see the Queen about her ball."

The last time the royals had opened their doors to any and all, every character in the land had come with a whoop and come with a call—some in rags, some in jags, and some in velvet gowns.

If we wanted to keep things orderly, it was smart to increase police presence at the royal palace.

We entered the Happily Ever After Hills where picturesque castle turrets, spires, and rose-covered towers buttressed the horizon.

When we reached the castle's front gate, I knocked.

The Knave of Hearts opened the gate. He was lean and stern, his dark wavy hair a dead-match of Chuck's style. He wore black from the soles of his boots to the starched edge of his collar.

"Detectives." He crooked a short bow, letting daylight slip blades of amber into the folds of his clothing. "Please follow me. The Queen is waiting."

He turned, boots making no more noise than a cat on feathers. Muffet and I followed him.

The glittering halls were decorated with gilded art of mocking birds that won't sing, diamond rings set in brass, and of course, looking glass.

I'd once taken the Knave in for tasting the Queen's tarts on a summer day. The Queen had dropped the charges. Chic had printed a story in the Slinger accusing the Queen and Knave of a love affair.

The Queen had denied she and the Knave had ever done anything inappropriate. When pressed, the Knave had confirmed the same.

I'd never believed them. I wasn't the only one.

King Cole, who had long carried on a not-so-hidden affair with Bo Peep, immediately made the Knave his personal servant.

I figured it was a worse punishment than if the king had just banished him from the royalty altogether.

But Cole kept friends close, and tart-stealers much, much closer.

It had taken a toll on the Knave. He used to be a kind-hearted laughing man, always up for a harmless prank or night of fun.

Now he was solemn as a Grundy, silent as a night, and always wore black.

We passed doors open to sitting rooms, galleries, straw-spinning halls, and other pastimes only the royals could afford.

The Knave led us to a smaller chamber and knocked on the gold door carved with flamingos bent into the shape of hearts.

"Enter," a woman commanded from the other side of the door.

The Knave pulled a soft breath and drew his shoulders back. If he looked neutral and disinterested before, he somehow found a way to look even more bored. He entered the room and held the door open for us.

"The Detectives Peter and Muffet," he announced, politely staring at the red velvet wallpaper instead of at the ruby-bedecked woman in the room.

I pulled off my hat. "Your Majesty." I bowed.

The Queen stood next to an ornate red and gold throne on a slightly raised dais.

"Detective," she replied icily. "What is the meaning of this outrage?"

CHAPTER 14

The Queen of Hearts was a stunning beauty, the kind of dame who didn't need a magic mirror to tell her she still had game.

With her red hair curled elaborately on top of her head, her willowy build, and nails filed sharp enough to draw blood, she looked like a rose: lovely and dangerous.

She wore a tidal wave of red—dress, shoes, silks, jewelry, crown—and a single egg-shaped green jewel the size of a fist, hanging on a silver chain.

I'd never seen her wear any jewel other than a ruby.

I'd never seen her smile.

I'd also never seen her clench copy of the Sixpence Slinger in her outstretched fist like a club.

"Outrage!" she repeated.

"Ma'am?" I asked. "Which outrage are you speaking of?"

"My ball," she said.

"The Prince's ball," Knave corrected under his breath.

She lobbed a scowl his way, but if he noticed, he didn't show it. "*My* royal ball," she went on, "is on the front page of this...this...gossip rag."

"I saw that," I said. "You didn't want the front page?"

The Knave didn't move, his gaze fixed on the wall across the room, but he did sigh.

"Of course I wanted the front page. *I* wanted it. Do you know who is doing all the work to throw this ball?"

"The staff?" Muffet asked.

The Knave coughed to cover a laugh.

"Yes," the Queen said, "the staff. But *I* am making all the decisions. I am guiding every choice, every color, every single moment. If it weren't for *me*, there wouldn't be a ball!"

The Knave coughed again. This time it definitely sounded like a laugh.

"Do you have something to add to the discussion, Knave?" she asked archly.

"I do not, Your Highness." Eyes forward. Posture straight. But his mouth had curved ever so slightly at the corners, and his voice mellowed to something some other Jack might call teasing.

He was enjoying this.

The Queen noticed it too. Her cheeks colored pink, and for a moment, I thought she might actually smile.

"See it remains that way," she said instead. "You, Detective." She snapped the paper so the front page was visible. "Solve this."

I had no clue what the problem was. She'd gotten a full-front, full-color treatment with a big headline in red, her favorite color.

"She's not on..." the Knave whispered.

"You're not on it," Muffet said.

The Queen's gaze took her in from beret to boots. "Who are you, again?"

"Miss Muffet, Ma'am."

"Do you know my story?"

"Yes, Ma'am. Everyone knows your story."

"Everyone knows what is written. But surely, I am more than just a woman who bakes tarts."

Muffet pressed her lips together and nodded slightly.

"Story and duty," the Queen went on, "are good and well, but I am *royalty*. I deserve to be seen. I deserve to have what I want, how I want it, when I want it. I have always deserved that."

I would argue that being royalty gave her all those things, story or no story.

"This is *my* ball," the Queen insisted. "I demand *my* picture appear on the front page."

I cleared my throat trying to decide how to tell her if wishes were horse, then beggars wouldn't have to walk. "We don't have any pull with the paper, Your Majesty."

"This," she clenched the paper. "Is a crime. Does the law have any pull with criminals, Detective?"

The door behind us swung open.

There in the arch was King Cole, the jolly old soul himself.

Old was a misnomer for this man. He'd gotten the name due to an unfortunate mispronunciation during his rhyme writing.

The tellers back then had intended to start his rhyme with a flourishing "Oh." Someone heard it wrong and slipped an "ld" in there, causing "Oh, King Cole was a merry old soul," to become, "Old King Cole."

Back when he'd gotten his rhyme and taken over the kingdom, he'd been a youngster. He'd liked the idea of being older and wiser than everyone else.

He'd liked it enough he'd never allowed his story be rewritten. And since he alone carried the keys to the Goose's Vault in the Wood where the Book was kept, his story never changed.

Cole was the opposite of the Knave: light haired and ruddy skinned, his beard cut tight. His golden ringlets shone like the sun and could make Goldilocks give up her gig.

He was ox-shouldered and heavily muscled beneath a layer of soft living.

The near-permanent smile he wore wasn't so much jolly as eager to get on with the cruelty of the day.

"Knave, Queen," he said, "What are you both doing here? Together? Without my permission?"

There was something beneath the mild tone that squirmed like an early bird's buffet. The Knave and Queen heard it too.

The Knave held statue-still, his face blank as the King prowled into the room.

The Queen went a startling shade of white. "I thought you were riding," she exhaled as if her lungs had failed her. "You were supposed to be riding today." Her gaze cut to the key ring at his belt, then at the Knave, then back to the keys.

"When there is a ball to plan?" He strode across the room. The key ring holding the only key to the Goose's Vault, chimed softly with each step.

"When you are making *plans* without my consult?" He took the stairs to the dais and would have walked right through her, if the Queen hadn't stepped to one side.

"*I* am the King here. *I* rule this land and control

every story in it." He settled his bulk onto the throne, his hands spread over the armrests.

"But I saw your horse," the Queen said. "I saw a rider. Your purple cape."

Cole waved his hand in the air dismissively. "The Prince is hunting for a fearsome beast. My mighty charger and royal cape are the best in the land. Of course I want the Prince to have the best in the land."

"You were supposed to be on your ride," she breathed. "Your daily ride."

"How do you know when I ride?"

"I..." She drew herself up. "I am the Queen. Should I not know?"

"No," he said, "you should not. My business and schedule are my own. I have never shared either with you."

The Queen went silent, staring through him as if she couldn't see him, the room, or maybe the world.

"You cruel, cruel fool—" she choked. Then she turned and ran from the room.

CHAPTER 15

"Come, come," Cole said gesturing Muffet and I closer. "What more do you need to know about the royal ball? My guest list is impressive, my food will be the best in the land, my musicians unparalleled."

"We need to know your security concerns," I said. "Every member of the force will be here to keep an eye out for trouble. The royalty's safety will be our highest priority."

"Of course it will."

"A list of people who have complaints with the royals would help us..."

He waved for silence. "Pipe!"

But if I was in for the penny, I was in for the pounding. "Your Majesty, we know the royal family has enemies."

Cole's eyes hardened with a warning.

Muffet got in the boat to take a turn at rowing. "The royal in-laws and wicked step-mothers, have caused more trouble than all the common folk together," she said.

"So to provide the best security, we'll need—"

"Bowl!" The King bellowed, ignoring us both and glaring at the door.

The Knave walked in—I hadn't heard him leave—carrying a silver platter with a gold-inlaid pipe and bowl.

He bumped into my shoulder briefly as he passed me and offered an apology. He stopped at the first stair of the dais and performed a stiff bow.

"Bring my pipe and bowl it here, you idiot," the King demanded.

The Knave strode up the dais and offered the King the contents of the platter.

Cole leaned forward and grunted. "Where is my alabaster pipe?"

"Your Majesty broke it this morning when Your Majesty heard the Queen had planned the perfect ball without you."

The King's eyes went round as a ragged rascal, his red face ruddy as a ragged rock. "Replace it. Now!" He shoved the platter.

The Knave's quick reflexes kept the priceless pipe and bowl from falling to the ground.

"Out!" The king ordered.

The Knave met the King's glare with a hush-a-bye calm. "Perhaps Your Majesty would care for a cigarette?" The Knave flicked his hand and a cigarette appeared between his fingers.

I was the only Joe in town who smoked that brand. I patted the pack in my pocket. Two cigarettes missing.

The Knave had fast fingers. He'd also just proved he could still get away with something right under the King's nose.

"Out!" Cole stabbed a finger at the door. "Fool! Thief! Go find a Pied Piper and follow him off a cliff!"

Muffet and I tensed, ready to break up a fight. But the Knave bowed to the King, bowed to Muffet and me. Then, with a slip of a smile, left the room.

I cleared my throat. The tension in the room was custard-thick. "We just need some information."

Cole sat back, and mopped sweat off his face. "I hired that cad when the Slinger smeared the Queen's good name. They said he was 'stealing her tarts.' They said she loved him. *Him*! A Knave. A fool! I rule this land and every story within it—including hers. Who would want that...that liar and thief when they had me? The King!"

I didn't give him the obvious answer: maybe the Queen did love the Knave. Maybe he loved her back. But they were required to live out their stories the way they were written. Stories he, the King, had the key to. Stories he, the King, could help rewrite.

Stories he, the King, refused to change.

He could make Las Fables a better place. He could change people's lives for the better. He had that power.

Too bad he liked having the power more than he liked doing anything good with it.

"We don't need information on the Knave, Your Highness," Muffet said. "We want a list of any new hostiles."

"New?" he scoffed. "There is nothing new in Las Fables. Every story remains the same, will *always* remain the same so long as I am King and the Book is in my control. As the Goose intended. Las Fables' stories will never change."

"Well, except for the Dwarves," Muffet said.

Gotta love a gal who told the truth, just the truth, nothing but the truth.

"What did you say?"

She shrugged. "The Seven Dwarves were murdered. Their story will need to be rewritten. That seems like a pretty big change to Las Fables."

He drew himself up, fingers clenching the arms of the throne.

"The Seven Dwarves are minor stories at best. Little people. Their story will remain as it is. No one will even notice."

I bumped Muffet's shoulder and stepped forward before she could counter that Snow White, for one, had already noticed their deaths. As had the Sins.

"Thank you for your time, Your Majesty," I said. "If there is any information on new threats we should be aware of, please let us know."

"There will be no new information. This ball will be no different than any other ball, Detective. Understood?"

"Yes, Your Majesty." I tapped Muffet's elbow. We bowed to the King and skedaddled out of there.

It didn't take long to beat it out into the brighter light of day.

"Nothing different." Muffet exhaled through her teeth. "Seven people are dead. Snow White was kidnapped. That's different. Can't he see that?"

I scrubbed at my eyes and fought a yawn. "The King has the luxury of not having to see the real world. We're the sailors who have to see see see, from the sky to the bottom of the great blue sea sea sea."

She made a sound that might have been agreement. "So what's next?"

"We call in everyone who can help with security. Make sure we've one-two'd, buckled our shoes before we three-four, shut the doors."

"Can do, Boss."

I tried and failed to cover another yawn.

"You been up two days straight now," she said as we followed the cobbled streets.

The breeze shifted, and I caught the cinnamon sweetness of her perfume mixed with a tantalizing whiff of bug spray. My pulse did a rumba, even though a guy like me didn't have the kind of moves it took to dance with a skirt like her.

But maybe a guy like me just needed to hold his hand out and risk it. Risk asking for a turn around the room. I let my thoughts waltz with that pleasant image.

"When are you going to get some down time?" she asked.

I blinked. I'd lost track of time and trail. We were already a few blocks from the station.

"Later. Today. Maybe."

She placed her hand on my elbow and stopped walking. I took the cue and faced her.

She was close enough, her head tipped up, I could kiss her without having to do anything more than lean down to her mouth. Would she taste like honey? Spice? Everything nice?

"When, maybe?" she asked.

Everything in me said *now, maybe. Forever, maybe.*

But my responsibility was still only story and duty. She was talking about me getting rest, not starting a dance, a life with her.

"Maybe when Las Fables isn't crawling with crime

and murderers." I couldn't seem to take my gaze off her bare throat, her soft mouth, her forest eyes.

"Wouldn't that be a nice sort of maybe? No crime in Las Fables." She smiled one of her killer smiles. "How about we start with breakfast, maybe?"

"Too much work to do. Setting up security for the ball..."

"That won't take all day."

"No, I suppose not."

The birds were bob-bob-bobbing along as they flew by, the song calling sunlight out from behind clouds.

Muffet looked good in sunlight. Muffet looked good in any light.

"Then we have time for breakfast," she said. "You and me, Paddy Cake's. As soon as we get security sorted for the ball. Deal?"

She didn't turn, but started walking away from me backward, sunlight threading gold through her yellow hair.

Even a chump like me couldn't refuse an offer like that. "Deal," I said, following her.

"Good." She turned and picked up the pace. "It's a date."

CHAPTER 16

I called in every security guard, police officer, and watch in the town, then got down to hammering brass tacks. We'd done security for the royals before. But I didn't agree with King Cole.

Something *was* different about Las Fables.

Something was new.

There was an edge to the air. Sharp enough to prick a finger and send a whole castle to dreamland.

My gut said something serious was about to go down, and I was going to make sure we were ready for it.

By the time I'd handed out assignments to officers and volunteers, I was energized, geed up. We were as ready as we could be for anyone or anything that tried to get the bulge on the ball.

A knock rapped at my doorframe and I looked up from the paperwork.

"Hey, Boss," Muffet said. "Got a minute?"

I leaned back in my chair. "Sure. What do you need?"

"Lunch."

"All right."

"With you," she said.

I opened my mouth, but she beat me to the punch. "The plan was breakfast, but I'll settle for lunch for our date."

"Date." I stared at the papers spread across my desk, then rubbed the back of my neck. "About that..."

She rested a shoulder against the door jamb. "You gonna stand me up, Boss? Really?"

"There's work—"

"There's always going to be work. This lunch is a one-time offer."

That smile looked a lot like a challenge and a little like flirting. Before I could over-think it, I stood. "I have a lot of work to do."

"You always do."

"I don't have much time."

"We'll eat fast." She winked and all my arguments disappeared.

"Paddy's?" I asked.

"What a great idea. Where did you get that great idea?"

"Ha-ha," I said. I plucked my coat and hat from the hook and gestured for her to proceed.

Just outside the station, a very-not-old man was nicknack paddy-whacking about giving his dog a bone. The dog in question lounged at his feet, the bowl next to it nearly filled with coins.

It was a story violation, against the codes to profit off someone else's rhyme. Only this *old* man could sing that song and give his dog a bone.

"Nice day," Muffet said, as we passed a batch of freshly baked, fancy frosted gingerbread men hauling sass down the street.

"I suppose," I said.

On the next corner, an *actual* old man crooned about playing nicknack on his thumb. That fit the story.

But the dog at his feet was a cat lounging in a small donation box with the words: Stones for Bones written on it.

Cat didn't fit the story. I scowled and thought about issuing a ticket.

"Nice weather, nice walk, nice scenery," Muffet said.

I grunted, which made her chuckle.

"Let me guess." She rocked close enough our arms almost brushed with each step. "You're making a list of all these buskers' violations of code and want to ticket every one of them."

"If I see one more non-regulation old man playing nicknack paddy-wack without a permit, there's going to be consequences."

That got one sharp, delighted giggle out of her. Then she pressed her fingers over her mouth. "Oh no," she said between her fingers.

She pointed.

Just ahead, a woman in a fake beard and eyepatch threw herself into a double cartwheel and yelled, "...this old man went rolling home!"

"That one doesn't even have a dog," Muffet said.

"I see that."

Her smile flashed bright, the laughter clear in her voice. "You want me to issue a warning? A ticket? You want me to book 'em?"

I want you to stay happy, I thought.

I want you to be the one doll in my life who doesn't play me for a rube.

I want to know if a limerick like me has a chance with a sonnet like you.

"Maybe after lunch," I grumbled, which made her smile wider. I was starting to like that I could make her smile.

"All right," she said. "You're sure you don't need me to do anything else for you, Boss?"

A whole list of things she could do for me sprang to mind. My pulse kicked up a beat.

"Is this what it looks like?" I asked, opening the door to Paddy's Diner for her.

"What does it look like?"

"It looks like you're flirting with me."

And oh, the smile she gave me. "Amazing powers of observation, Detective."

She sashayed into the diner, and nothing in the land could stop me from following her.

She settled at one of the open booths by the window—the same booth where Horner and I usually had breakfast—and picked up the menu.

"Look at that," she said. "They have sugar, and spice, and everything nice today. Just like every day."

I took the seat opposite her. I had the menu memorized but picked it up to give my hands something to do.

"You like spice, Boss?" she asked not looking at me.

"I do."

"You like hot buns?" This time her gaze flicked up, twinkling.

It was hot in the joint. How had it gotten so hot? I tugged at my collar.

"Peter!" Paddy called out as he rounded the counter and stopped by our table. "Good to see you. And Miss Muffet, what a delight. Can I get you some tea? Curds and whey?"

"Oh, I'm going for something more adventurous today, thanks," she said.

Paddy frowned. "You? But, curds and whey..." He was flummoxed that she might order something outside her story.

He wrung his hands and looked around as if needing help.

"You know what?" She put the menu down. "Please bring me curds and whey. *And* bring me a bit of bitter butter and a plate of hot crossed buns."

The frown lifted and he seemed relieved. "Curds and whey, with a side of buns, can do. Peter? Pumpkin?"

Muffet folded her hands and watched me expectantly. It looked like she was daring me to order outside my normal too.

"I'll have what she's having," I said.

Paddy nodded. "Pumpkin and a side of buns. Comin' up."

Muffet watched him go and shook her head. "Every time," she said.

"Every time what?"

"He thinks I want curds and whey."

I shrugged. "It's your story."

She tipped her head. "It is. What do you think about that?"

"I think we have to stay sharp before the ball. The Dwarves' murder might give other criminals ideas."

"You brought me on a lunch date, our *first* date, and you want to talk about work?"

"It's not that I don't want…I've thought about…" I waved my hand between her and me, "but we don't have time…"

"For living?" She tucked a strand of hair behind her ear but missed one golden tendril that snaked down the curve of her neck and pooled near her collarbone.

I wanted to touch her. Wanted to feel the silk of that spun gold in my palm.

"For anything other than solving the case," I heard myself say. "Cases. Something about the Old Woman's confession feels hinky. The Dwarves, the Sins, the Prince hunting a Nary Tale. Las Fables is falling apart. It's our job to build it up again. Keep it safe. Story and duty."

"We'll do our jobs," she said. "We're good at this kind of thing. But life is going to happen whether we solve the cases fast or slow."

"We'll solve them fast," I said.

She studied my face. "You know we have—lulls. We have time when it isn't just story or duty. What we do between solving cases," she waved between us, mimicking me, "who we spend that time with…isn't that what makes life worth living?"

"Our stories make life worth living." It was an automatic response, said as I was taught to say.

But sitting with a dame I respected, a dame I wanted to spend time with on cases, before cases, after cases, those diamond words turned to brass.

"Sure." She slipped the smile back into place, but it wasn't the same.

"Muffet, I—"

"It's fine." She shrugged. "I just think there's more to life than the story written for us. I think we could change our story. Maybe even rewrite some of it. I know that's wishing-on-a-star kind of talking."

The Goose had chosen how we would live. The stories she wrote for us were the guiding lights we were required to abide by. Her stories kept our world orderly and safe.

For whom? my treacherous mind asked.

Somewhere in the distance, I heard a storm wind rising, gyre and gimbling in the wabe.

But even as I knew I should only have story and duty tapp-tapping on my brain, my thoughts strayed again and again to the woman in front of me.

The red dress.

The laughter.

The hopeful look in her eyes that made me want to say yes, no matter what the question might be.

I opened my mouth to tell her maybe we could both wish upon some stars, when Paddy glided up to the table.

"Pumpkin for Peter, curds for Muffet. Just how you like it, how you'll always like it!"

He dropped the dishes onto the table.

"Just how we'll always like it," Muffet repeated

staring at the meal like it was writing on the wall she had to accept. She took a determined spoonful.

Whatever star I'd almost wished upon winked out, and was gone.

CHAPTER 17

After lunch, Muffet and I took the road less traveled back to the station, going over the hill and far away toward the Tulgey Wood.

The hill wasn't very high, but we paused at the top to enjoy the view and immediately wished we hadn't.

"Oh," Muffet said.

The land below was bare.

Once, the Tulgey Wood had stood resplendent, the mighty red-and-orange limbed Tumtum trees covered in leaves of blue, purple, and the strange pastel colors of old Nary Tales.

But not a tree or mulberry bush remained.

Instead, the land was covered by a structure that looked like a town unto itself. Turrets, pavilions, and snail shell spiraled walkways glittered in the morning light. It was a glitzy scab sparkling over a fresh wound.

A banner across the road read: MALLBERRY'S GRAND OPENING

"I'd heard Snow gave the Pigs the Dwarves' corner of the Tulgey Wood," Muffet said, "but I didn't know they'd cut down so much more."

"Pigs build faster than a wolf can huff." I eyed the half dozen witches circling the air above the plaza. "Let's check it out."

The scent of gingerbread, pocket rye, and coffee mixed with the zing of happy citizens wandering the streets. Las Fables had turned out in droves to buy a bit of finery for the upcoming ball.

On one side of the street, green-hatted elves hawked shoes good enough for the King while in the shop opposite, the stylish "wonder thread" boys spun cloth only royalty could see.

A short crabapple of a man grabbed my hand and shook it hard.

"WelcomePeter!Welcome! Doyourememberme? RipWinkle. CanIgetyoucoffee? OfcourseIcan."

He darted back behind a sinister-looking contraption of copper and dials that took up most of his small shop. He twisted and tweaked until the machine steamed, and thick, dark coffee poured into tiny cups.

"Rip?" Last I'd seen him, he'd been a slow-eyed narcoleptic professional bowler. "Is that you Van Winkle?"

He laughed, a high tittering sound. "Ofcourse it'sme!"

"What happened to bowling?" Muffet asked. "I thought you were working for that thunder trophy."

"Stillam. Justdoingcoffee ontheside. Roastedandripped. Gonnaget rich. Cream?"

"Black's fine," I said accepting the tiny cup with the word Ripped scrawled across it in red.

Muffet took the other cup and sipped. "Strong," she wheezed. "You like this set up so far?" She tipped her chin toward the huge shopping space.

Rip shifted from foot to foot like he had a candle lit under each shoe. His gaze skittered beneath his storm cloud of wild hair. "It'snotsobad. Witchesdon'tlikeit."

"Don't like the Pigs?" she asked.

"Don'tlikewhat theydid. CuttingdowntheTulgey."

That made sense. Not every witch lived in the Wood, but every one of the old gals needed space for her chicken-legged hut or delicious candy house. Losing the Wood limited their living spaces.

Witches and Pigs had been fighting for years over how the Wood should be used. Giving the Pigs the Dwarves' portion of the land hadn't helped matters.

A loudspeaker crackled and the littlest pig, Straw, cleared his throat. The sound cut through the crowd. "Thank you all for coming," he squealed.

"What do I owe you for the coffee, Rip?" I asked.

"Onthe house, Peter. Onthehouse. Youtwocomeby anytime."

"Will do." I nodded to Muffet, and we sewed through the crowd like a needle pulling thread.

"We are glad to have you here at the grand opening of Mallberry's," Straw squeaked.

A crowd gathered in a wide courtyard with a fountain in the center. In front of the fountain was a raised platform. On that stood the Three Pigs.

They were on their back hooves and dressed in fine vests, each of them a couple hundred pounds of money-hungry, land-grabbing, rent-raising pork.

Straw handed the microphone to his taller, darker brother, Sticks.

"For today only," Sticks said in a deeper grunt, "we are offering a commemorative straw, stick, or brick for each citizen. One lucky shopper will win a brand-new vehicle!"

He held up a pumpkin and a little cage with four white mice in it. A vial of INSTANT HORSES was tied to the side with a red ribbon.

The applause grew and the crowd moved closer to the fountain to claim their free building materials.

The witches were in the crowd now, brooms in hand, familiars—cats, toads, weasels, beetles—riding their shoulders.

Sticks moved out of the way, and Bricks, the brute of the family, stepped up to the mic.

He was dark gray and bristly from snout to hoof, a tattoo of a dead wolf on his shoulder. Rumor said his daddy was a razorback who'd motored through town, stole his mama's heart, emptied her bank account, and motored out again.

Bricks was a lot like his daddy—heartless and greedy. When he spotted the witches in the crowd, his beady eyes narrowed.

"People of Las Fables," he grunted. "The boys and me are here to give you anything you need. This," he stretched his short arms and waved at the plaza, "is a new start. You need for anything, we'll get it for you.

"We Pigs will devote our every breath to making your wishes come true. I mean, it's not like the witches have been doing you any favors lately, am I right?"

The witches rolled up sleeves, brandished brooms, and strong-armed their way to the fountain.

"Wolves! Dirt! Scum!" they yelled as they marched.

The crowd shuffled to make room for the old gals, but the Pigs didn't budge.

"You tore down our houses!" a witch shrieked.

"You flattened the Tulgey Wood!" another wailed.

"You took our tricks and treats and burned our trails! Where will the children get lost with their breadcrumbs?"

"Ladies," Straw said, "we've been over this. We own the land now. It was given to us fair and square."

"Not from us! We didn't give it to you!"

"The land wasn't yours, you bunch of squatters," Sticks said.

"It's part of our story!"

"To spell with your story," Bricks growled. "We got ours. Now you can get lost."

As one, the women in black raised their wands and pointed them at the Pigs. The crowd scattered faster than gingerbread fresh out of the oven.

Muffet and I pushed our way through the crowd, trying to get to the witches before they did something the Pigs would regret.

"Wait!" a woman's voice rang out across the plaza.

The crowd stopped. All eyes turned to her.

She was slender and tall, her hair tucked beneath a tightly fitting black head cover over which she wore a large black witch's hat. She cut a figure in a long black dress and heavy black cape.

The only spark of color on her was a green stone amulet suspended on a silver chain.

There was something familiar about the witch. Something powerful that twigged my instincts. But every time I tried to get a look at her face, my gaze skittered away.

She was using magic, hiding her face in plain sight. Which meant she was not what she seemed to be.

"She's using magic," Muffet said. "Powerful magic."

I thought I knew every spell slinger in town. But I didn't know one who could pull off this kind of magic.

"We can resolve our differences." She nodded toward the witches. "A peaceful resolution, sisters."

The witches grumbled but lowered their wands.

"You recognize her?" I asked Muffet.

"I think I've seen her, but..." She frowned, fingers tapping the bug spray at her hips.

"How big of a resolution?" Sticks asked. From the way he said it, he wanted a resolution made of gold, and lots of it.

She glided through the crowd until she was in front of the podium, then rose up and hovered eye-to-eye with the Pigs.

"There is a patch of the Tulgey we witches most want. We will pay you handsomely for it."

She rolled her fingers and a treasure chest appeared at Straw's feet.

Bricks snorted. "Not for sale. That land is ours fair and square. If you don't like it, go cry to Judge White."

Straw opened the lid of the chest and gasped. He tapped Stick's arm.

Sticks glanced in the box, and his eyes bulged. He tugged on Brick's arm.

"You will find our offer very generous," she said. "*Very.*"

Muffet and I worked around a few of the larger

black hats, trying to get a look at what was in that chest, but couldn't get an angle on it.

Bricks lumbered over to the chest and dropped a hoof on the edge of it, tipping it forward just slightly.

I caught a glimpse of boxes, the kind small pies might fit inside, before he let his hoof fall. He squinted at the witch.

"All right," he said. "You want something, we want something. Come back to our office. Let's talk."

"Oh, that's not suspicious at all," Muffet said.

"We're going to be a part of that discussion," I replied.

But before I could make my move, I heard a shout.

"Peter," Horner called as he ran our way. "Trouble!"

The witches muttered and grumbled, but stowed their wands. "No trouble," I said. "We've got a handle on the ing-bing."

"Not the witches," Horner said. "Something worse." He grabbed hold of my shoulder, breathing hard. "Someone tried to kill Chuck Charming."

My gut fell like a boy from a beanstalk.

CHAPTER 18

"What do we know?" I asked Horner as we ran. "Just the facts."

"Chuck was returning from the Tulgey Wood," Horner said. "Hunting the Jabberwock. The King's horses were coming back from the smithy—getting nails in their shoes replaced."

"All the pretty little horses?" Muffet asked.

Horner nodded. "The horses found him."

"They called it in?" I asked.

"Yes."

"Doctor?" I asked, as we took the fork in the road to the scene of the crime.

"Foster," Horner said. "Was in a puddle—"

"—up to his middle," I said. I knew his story as well as he did.

Horner swallowed. "Right. One of the horses

pulled him out and took him to the Prince. The horses were afraid to move Chuck."

Good choice. After the Humpty accident where the horses made a mess of the poor egg, it was good to know they were trying to be a little more cautious.

"Bears?" Muffet asked.

"Already called for them," Horner said.

With the hoof traffic that must have scuffled the crime scene, I wasn't sure even the Three Bears could pull a clue out of the mess.

"Is Chuck going to be okay?" I asked.

Horner didn't answer. He just pointed.

We had rounded the bend in what was once the Tulgey Wood.

There lay Chuck Charming, face down, battered and bleeding.

A cold chill duck-duck-goosed down my spine. I took a breath.

Change. Las Fables was changing.

The Dwarves were dead.

The Sins had taken Snow.

The Pigs were building where no pig had built before.

And now, Chuck, the Prince, the TDH, the hero of one of the greatest stories in all Las Fables, had fallen.

"Peter," Muffet's voice was solid as a rock crushing scissors, "he's alive."

I reassessed the scene.

Brush and weeds were pulverized, the ground trampled. A score of the King's horses stood by, staring at the Prince in equine horror.

Las Fables might be changing. But it hadn't croaked yet.

Muffet squeezed my arm then stepped back.

"Detective Peter, Detective Muffet," Dr. Foster called out. "Your assistance, please."

Foster wasn't a tall man, but he carried himself with authority. His normally doughy face was tired, worried, as if he'd just played roll-over with a bed full of bears. His hair stood out from his head in a dandelion puff of white. He was (predictably) damp from the waist down, the cuffs of his trousers dripping mud over practical shoes.

"Together," Foster said, taking position at the Prince's shoulders.

Horner crouched on the opposite side of Chuck's torso, I knelt on the other side, and Muffet bent near his ankles.

"We'll all roll him over onto his back and onto the stretcher," Foster said. "One smooth movement. And gently," he admonished even though not one of us had moved a muscle.

He three-two-one'd, and we carefully turned the Prince onto the stretcher.

"Interesting," Muffet said.

"Huh," Horner added.

I looked away from the Prince to study the Doctor's face.

"Well, Doc?" I asked.

"I've never seen wounds like this. They look like claw marks."

"They're glowing," I added.

The doctor studied the three long marks drawn from Chuck's right shoulder to left hip.

It was as if he had been snicker-snacked by his own vorpal blade—if his blade had been made of claws.

"He's breathing." Foster ran practiced hands over the Prince. "Otherwise seems stable. We can move him to the castle."

The horses gave a collective sigh of relief and nickered congratulations to each other.

"I'll need two horse volunteers."

Fifty hooves flew into the air. The doctor pointed at two random horses. "You two," he said, then to us, "Help me lift and secure the stretcher."

The horses got into position, and we hoisted the stretcher between them and attached it to the harnesses.

The doctor checked our work and rubbed at his chin. "He's in a deep sleep. It appears magical."

"Does he need a Prince to kiss him out of it?" Muffet asked.

"It will certainly be one of the first things we try,"

Foster said. "Then his true love, of course. After that, we'll move on to spells and witchery."

I nodded, knowing Chuck was in the best hands in Las Fables.

"We'll be by later, Doc," I said. "All you horses can form a line and trot off," I pointed, "that way."

The horses hurried to follow my directions, bumping into each other and churning up what was left of the crime scene as they cantered away.

I let out a sigh. Horses.

"What a mess," Horner muttered.

"You can say that again," an annoying voice announced. "Say cheese, Peter!" A camera flashed.

Chic, at the edge of the crime scene laughed and forwarded the film. "Your incompetence just made the front page. Again!"

"If you take one more step," Muffet said, advancing on the twerp of a reporter, "you will be contaminating a crime scene. And I will be forced to escort you out of here."

Chic popped his gum. "Mother, may I?" he taunted.

"Oh, you bet your butt, you may," she said. "Giant steps."

He took three exaggerated giant steps backward and snapped another photo.

"This is the line, Chic." Muffet pointed at the ground and swung her arm to indicate the edge of the churned dirt. "You stay on that side, and we'll have no problems."

"Sure, toots. Whatever you say. Wanna give me a quote? Is the Prince dead? Was it a revenge killing? A serial killer? Is Las Fables under attack?"

"This is a crime scene," she repeated, using that no-nonsense tone that shouldn't make me think about the kinds of nonsense I'd like to get into with her. "The Prince is alive. He's under the care of Doctor Foster. There is no known immediate danger to Las Fables. When we have more information, we will share it with the press."

Dame was a pro.

"Yeah, yeah." Chic smacked gum and meandered the perimeter of the clearing, the soles of his shoes almost, but not quite crossing the line Muffet had drawn.

Muffet caught my gaze and rolled her eyes. She could handle Chic with both bug sprays tied behind her back.

"Let's get this cordoned off," I said.

Horner and I staked off the clearing with police tape, ignoring Chic and his camera and his jeers.

Just as we tied down the last stake, the Three Bears rambled up the path.

"Pa, Ma, Junior," I said. "This might be a hard job."

Ma grumbled, a deep sound in her furry chest. "They're all hard jobs, Detective. Leave it to us."

She and Pa got busy sniffing, while Junior stopped and snapped photos, making his way slowly toward the center.

Horner jotted notes in his sketch book and Muffet had her eye on Chic. I stepped outside the police tape and lit a cigarette. I scanned the area, looking for a sign of where the attacker may have gone.

The road forked away from here, one path nice and clean, the other less traveled. It was overgrown with weeds, brambles, and knobby-fingered tree roots.

There was another road, really no more than a footpath, barely visible in the undergrowth. I took that less-than less than traveled path down the hill, away from town and Mallberry's, past a brook, a rocky pile.

A flock of four-and-twenty black birds crossed overhead, their shadow shaped like a slice of pie cut through the path in front of me.

They squawked and cawed as they flew, singing a barbershop quartet song about kings and wishes and dainty dishes.

Then they fell silent.

Everything went silent.

Could be nothing.

Could be a granny-hungry wolf passing by.

A giant looking for bones for his bread.

A horseman with no head hunting an terrified crane.

But when the wind picked up, it carried a low,

slow, *whiffle*. A whiffle that should not exist in Las Fables.

I held very still, scanning the nothing to my right and emptiness to my left. The wind shifted again, drawing sticks and stones like a clatter of bones. The whiffle was gone.

The blackbirds picked up their song by the fork full, by the beak full.

Nary Tales, scary tales, weren't true. Not in Las Fables.

Until maybe they were.

CHAPTER 19

I returned to the crime scene. "Anything yet?" I asked Horner.

Ma Bear scratched a claw behind her ear and pulled down a small pair of reading glasses, balancing them on her nose. She fished paper out of her apron pocket and peered at it.

"The attacker wasn't too small, or too medium," she said. "It was too big. Much too big for Prince Charles to defeat."

"What kind of weapon did the attacker have?"

"Too hard to tell," Pa said. "The cut foliage means it was too sharp, not too dull. A big knife, a small sword, a medium claw."

"Can you tell which way he went?"

Pa shook his huge head, sending a fly and bumble

bee to fiddle-dee-dee up into the air. "The trail is not hot. It is not warm."

"You're saying it's cold," I said.

"Too cold," Pa agreed. "Nothing to follow."

"Horses," Horner complained.

Muffet had Chic locked in a stare-down several more giant steps away from the edge of the clearing.

"Honey!" Junior piped. "He dropped to all fours and rambled over to a large rose bush.

Horner and I followed, the bear parents behind us.

Junior reached into the rose bush and pulled out a piece of cardboard, like a bit of a small box, about the size of my palm. The cardboard was wrapped in spun sugar.

"Sticky," Junior said.

Horner took the paper from the bear.

"Not honey or sugar," he said, turning it carefully. "It's some kind of silk thread, a mimsy cocoon."

"Spider problems around here?" I asked.

"Nope!" Muffet called from halfway across the clearing. She might not be able to hear all of our conversation, but she never missed someone talking about spiders.

Horner passed the clue to me, and I held it to the light. I couldn't make out anything more useful, so I dropped it into an evidence bag. I handed that to Ma Bear.

"Finish up here, Bears, then bring everything you

have to the station," I said. "Tonight would be better than morning."

"You working tonight?" Pa bear asked.

"When a citizen has been attacked, I work every night."

Pa grunted and went back to sniffing the crime scene.

Muffet was, once again, listing off the reasons why one particularly annoying reporter wasn't allowed past the police tape.

She stood with her hands on her belt, her chin tipped like she had a bug in her sight and was ready to send it packing.

Chic, who was currently that bug, shouted, "Fine!"

He huffed and puffed away, muttering about deadlines and unhelpful no-comment cops.

Muffet tipped her head toward each shoulder, cracking her neck, then strolled our way.

"Everything Jake?" I asked.

"He got his story," she said. "When there's more, he'll get more. What's our move, Boss?"

The wind blew cold, stealing away the warmth of the day. We had a lot of pots and kettles on the fire. I flicked my smoke to the ground and called the shots.

"Horner and I will check in on the royals," I said. "You head back to the station. See if any information has come in on Chuck's attack, or the Pigs and witch situation at Mallberry's."

"Or the Dwarves' murder," she said, with what I guessed was an imitation of my voice. "Or the Sins kidnapping. And start the paperwork, Muffet."

The smile was still there, just a tuck at the corner of her mouth. She was giving me the raz but wasn't really mad about it.

"And *finish* the paperwork, Muffet," I instructed, which made her smile grow. I fought down a grin.

Horner cleared his throat.

"Maybe you and Muffet would like to check in on the royals together," he suggested.

Muffet shook her head. "Not when there's mountains of paperwork waiting for me. That'll keep me busy for hours."

I opened my mouth to ask why I couldn't keep her busy for hours, but Horner bumped my shoulder and got me walking toward the castle instead of staring at the dame.

"You finally ask her out?" he asked.

"No."

He gave me a hard look and heat hit my face. "She asked me," I mumbled.

He lit up like a lamp lighter on fire. "It's about time! How did it go?"

How did I explain that sitting with her over lunch had been one of the best experiences in my life?

How did I tell him her wishful ideas about story— that we could somehow be more than what was written for us—spoke to me in a way I'd never known before?

How did I explain that just hearing her laugh made my joints go loose and my body so light I thought I could fly?

I said, "Fine."

He made a sound halfway between a laugh and a snort. "Maybe more than fine?"

"Maybe."

We'd made it back to the city. The shops and houses sported candy roofs, tended gardens, and cobbled walkways.

"You and Blue?" I asked.

It was Horner's turn to go a little cherry in the cheek, only he did it with a grin. "Yeah. I asked him out. He's running his mom's bar now. Turned it into a jazz joint. You should hear him play, Peter. He's amazing."

I grunted, but really, I was pleased for him. "Sounds like you're onto a good thing there."

"He's a plum," he said.

"He feel the same about you?"

"I think so."

"Good." Their stories shouldn't keep them apart. Even though Blue might fall asleep when keeping sheep and cows, there was nothing to stop him from blowing his horn or falling in love. Unlike my story.

...had a wife and couldn't keep her...

I pushed away the words of my life. There was nothing I could do to change them anyway.

A gust of wind rippled down the street, stirring bits of litter and leaves. I paused, listening for a *whiffle*.

Horner stopped a few strides in front of me. "Peter?"

"Shh."

He waited, then asked. "You hear something?"

"No. Just the wind."

"What did you think you'd hear?"

I started walking again. This was where I tipped my mitt, and leveled with him. I expected he'd tell me I'd gone jingle brained. "I thought I'd hear a whiffle."

Horner slowed, then caught back up. "Do you hear it?"

"No."

"But...you've heard it before." It wasn't a question. I answered him anyway.

"Yes."

"Only one thing whiffles, Peter."

"I know." This was the moment where he told me I was a rube to believe in that kind of bunk.

"The Prince thought he heard it too," he said.

"I know."

We walked for a while in silence.

"Okay," he said. "I believe you."

Those words, coming from my partner meant more to me than any story in the Book.

CHAPTER 20

The Knave was pale as a goose and grim as the Brothers. "The Prince," he whispered, gripping the gate he held open for us.

"Alive?" Horner asked.

The Knave swallowed and nodded. "Yes. Thank the Goose, yes."

Horner visibly relaxed. "Good. That's good."

"We're here to see the King and Queen," I said. "We need every entrance and exit of the palace under guard."

"Of course." He ushered us through the castle.

Instead of taking us to a sitting room like before, he strode through golden bough and bramble wood halls, diamond and pearl encrusted ballrooms, and finally beneath two massive arched doorways into the most royal wing of the castle.

Here, the air took on a cooler touch, as if we were entering a museum.

The hush of our footsteps rose up to the carvings of fantastical creatures that decorated ceiling like frosting on a wedding cake.

We passed glass cases that held the famous story items: a single glass slipper, a spinning wheel spindle, and a golden plate with the rotten remains of a half-bitten apple on it.

Beyond the display of royal history, the marble hall opened to a corridor. Straight ahead was Chuck Charming's room.

"The King and Queen are within." Knave opened the door and stepped aside, letting us pass.

King Cole bulled out from the deeper shadows, ready for a fight. His eyes were wide, the blood drained from his face, leaving him as pasty as an undercooked muffin man.

"Detectives," he snapped. "Here." He jabbed a jeweled finger toward a receiving room.

We went where he pointed.

"Tell me everything you know about the attacker." He drew a black pipe out of his pocket, fingers trembling as he packed it with tobacco.

"We're still gathering information, Your Majesty," I said.

"Gather it faster," he ordered. "We've seen evil in this city, you and I."

"We have, Your Majesty," I agreed.

While Cole and I weren't exactly contemporaries and had never swum the same streams, I'd been there during the royal family's tougher times, including the recent kidnapping of Snow, and now, the attack on Charles.

Cole paced and puffed. "Giants, ogres, dragons, of course. The random wicked witch or two. But this isn't that, isn't any of those things. Who or *what* attacked Charles is…" He shook his head.

"What?" I asked. "Who do you think is behind this? Tell me everything. Who did Chuck hate? Who hated him back?"

Cole clamped teeth on the pipe and knit golden eyebrows. "He is a good man, Peter. My son."

"Good. Bad. I want to know who wants him dead."

The King exhaled cherry-scented smoke. His shoulders slumped, as if spite and rage had run out of steam.

He looked like a father who had seen his child bleeding beneath white sheets and couldn't do anything about it.

"You must find out who did this," said the man who was King. "Bring the attacker to justice. Because if you don't, I will find him, cut off his head, and put it on ice until you arrive."

So much for running low on spite and rage. "We'll find his attacker," I promised.

"Story and duty, Detective," he commanded.

"Story and duty," I repeated. "May we see the Queen?"

He motioned us to follow at his heels and took us into the bedroom proper.

I didn't know what I expected. Maybe a candle-light death vigil. Maybe weeping. Certainly sorrow. But the room was fully lit, the fire roaring merrily, the candles wicked up to full power.

The lavish bedroom was filled with couches, tables, desks, bookshelves, tapestries, and portraits of Chuck and Snow's life, from their first, coffin-date-gone-good to their royal wedding.

Other pictures of Chuck with his hunting trophies and Snow in her judge's robe adorned the walls.

But it was the Queen, resplendent in red from ruby crown to the tips of her scarlet gloves, who was the true work of art in the room.

She sat at a round table near the fireplace, sorting what looked like plants and potion bottles, the egg-sized green gem necklace glittering in the candlelight.

"Have you caught the brigand who harmed my son?" she asked without looking up.

"No, Ma'am. But we will."

"I will not tolerate my children being harmed. No mother would." Her gaze when she glanced my way would give Frosty freezer burn.

"Yes, Your Majesty. We're here to go over plans for your protection."

"My protection?"

"You and all the royals. I'd like to get guards in place immediately."

"If you think it will do any good," she said dismissively, going back to her potions.

Horner took a single step forward, notebook in hand. "I'd like to go over our plans, Your Majesty. With both Your Highnesses."

Cole moved to sit near the Queen. "You may approach," he said.

While Horner gave them the low down, I ambled to the other side of the room where heavy drapes shielded Chuck's bed.

I pulled aside the curtain and stepped into the darker space.

The four-poster bed was big enough for a three-headed giant. A single candle burned on the table by the bed, casting the occupant, velvet coverlets, and curtains in deep shadows.

Doctor Foster was slumped in a chair near the head of the bed, snoring softly.

I started toward him, but movement against the curtains stopped me in my tracks.

The Knave leaned into the space, carefully staying out of the royals' line of sight. He noticed me and would have scrammed if I hadn't caught his wrist.

His expression skipped a rope between sorrow and fear and touched the ground on defeat. I'd known the man for years. I'd never seen him so torn up—not even over the "tart-stealing" incident that had ended his affair, if not his feelings for the Queen.

I raised an eyebrow.

He whispered, "I have information."

Doctor Foster smacked his lips and stirred. The Knave's eyes went wide.

I leaned in. "Meet me by the Well."

He pressed a black leather-gloved hand on my shoulder in thanks, then slipped through the curtains and was gone.

"What?" Foster blinked blearily. "Who? Detective? Why are you here?"

"To check on the Prince," I said, stepping up to the head of the bed. "How is he?"

In the soft candlelight, Chuck's mouth was turned down in a brooding frown. His hair had never been fair like his father's, nor red like his mother's. With his dark hair and high, wide cheekbones giving his face that chiseled TDH look, Chuck really didn't resemble his father, the King, much at all.

He quite noticeably resembled the Knave. We all knew it. None of us spoke of it.

"He should recover." Foster heaved to his feet and stood on the opposite side of the bed, staring down at the sleeping Prince covered in luscious quilts.

"Not in time for the royal ball, though. But once he wakes, I expect him to regain full strength. As I said, we treated him with everything. Medicine, true-love's kiss, and healing spells."

"Good," I said. "What sort of weapon cuts like that, Doc? What could have made it glow?"

Foster's pebble-hard gaze glinted in the darkness, making me think of weasels and monkeys forever on the run.

"Do you want to know the truth, Detective?"

"Just the facts, Foster."

"Here are the facts." He leaned in as close as the bed between us would allow.

"I have seen every injury, means of torture, maiming, and gruesome death in this city. I have seen… everything our stories can do." His eyes were enormous and dark. "Charles' wounds were not made by any man, woman, or creature in Las Fables.

"Someone or some *thing* we've never seen before is stalking the land. It has a taste for royal blood now. But blood is blood. When it runs out of royals to attack, who do you think it will go after next?"

When I didn't answer, he leaned in, just that slight bit more.

"The streets are about to be bathed in blood, Detective. And none of us are going to come out of it alive."

CHAPTER 21

Horner and I hit the bricks. Evening was coming on soft, the moon a cat's grin, yellow and low in the dusky sky. I waited for the shadow of a bovine to cross it, but nothing happened.

I guess it was too early for the cows to come home.

"This way to the station is shorter," Horner said, pointing at a fork in the path.

"We're going to the Well."

"Why?"

"We have a man to meet."

"Who?"

"Knave."

"This ought to be interesting."

"I hope so."

A few rats squeaked a song in an alleyway, and

gingerbread men who had soaked up some early dinner rum staggered arm-in-arm down the sidewalk.

A little matchstick girl made of matchsticks—bare wooden feet and ready-strike head—tiptoed down the street. She snapped her stick fingers and flames caught between the sandpaper tips.

"Matches, matches!" she called as she blew out her fingers. "Matches for sale!" She leaned against the side of a building and pulled a small box of matches out of her pocket.

We passed the girl, following the road which opened upon a circular courtyard where half a dozen paths ended.

The little stone Wishing Well in the middle of the courtyard was the center of the city—the heart of Las Fables.

Here, it was rumored, wishes came true.

The houses that surrounded the courtyard were original old brick, two-story jobbers that teetered a bit, firelight glowing up the windows. Between the houses were plenty of trees, flowering vines, and garden gates.

Mary's Garden was across the courtyard. The curtained windows of that upscale bordello glowed in sensuous reds and pinks. Even though it was early, the sound of laughter and music drifted through the air.

A movement by the lemon tree caught my eye. The Knave slipped free of the shadows.

"Detectives." His voice was scuffed and soft.

"Knave," I said. "What part are you playing in all this?"

He did his own sky search for cows, cleared his throat, and closed the distance between us. He rested his hip against the Well.

"I didn't steal the Queen's tarts," he said. Then, quieter, "It was never her tarts that I wanted."

"That's in the past," I said. "She and Cole dropped the charges. What do you know about the attack on Chuck?"

"It wasn't supposed to happen this way."

Horner produced a notebook and took notes.

"How was it supposed to happen?" I asked.

Knave pinched the bridge of his nose. "I wasn't behind this. I didn't plan it. I definitely didn't want anything to happen to my...to Chuck. To the King's son."

That was as close as I'd ever heard him slip that Chuck was his. Cole had put the kibosh on that rumor real quick, and even though we all have eyes, Las Fables had kept its collective yap closed.

"All right," I said. "I'm listening."

"I was contacted by someone who wanted to stop the royal ball."

"Someone?"

"A sheep. A black sheep."

There was only one Black Sheep in Las Fables. A

double-crossing shady fellow who was always a hoof-step ahead of the law. He made a point of doing a lot of dirty work for whomever could keep his bags full.

I knew he was bad, but he was slippery too. I'd never had enough on him to keep him in shell for long.

"What did Baa-baa say?"

"I don't remember the exact words, but he said his boss wanted to make it inconvenient for the royal family to celebrate. Wanted to shake them up. Spook them. Just a scare, that's all. He said that was all."

"What did he want from you?"

"Schedules. He wanted to know when King Cole rode out into the woods, when he went to town, when he was sleeping, when he was awake. But only Cole's schedule. You have to believe me, Peter. I thought he wanted to scare Cole."

Cole, the man he hated most.

"What did you tell the sheep?"

"When Cole usually goes on his ride. I didn't know Chuck would be out." His voice dropped to a whisper. "I didn't know he would be wearing Cole's cape, riding Cole's horse."

"Who knows Cole's schedule besides you?" I asked.

"No one." He shook his head. "Not even the Queen."

"Who is Baa-baa working for?"

"I never wanted him hurt. I've been there since the

day he was born. He's a good, strong man. Not like the King. I hate Cole—you know that. You'd have to be blind as a mouse not to know how much I hate Cole, but Chuck…"

"Who was Baa-baa working for?" I asked again.

"I don't know. But he gave me this." Knave tugged a velvet bag out of his pocket. "Take it. I don't want it. I haven't used it. It's all there."

Horner accepted the bag and loosened the string. He tipped the contents onto his hand.

Rubies. Dozens of rubies. Enough dough Knave could have ridden off to live high on the hog, leaving servitude and Las Fables far behind him.

"Why are you still here?" I asked. "This could have bought you any horizon you wanted."

His eyes changed, fear and remorse replaced by hammer and steel. "I have reasons."

"The Queen?" Horner asked.

"Not how you're thinking."

"Then what?" I asked.

"Now that Chuck's grown?" His smile twisted. "I've stayed just to make Cole's life miserable."

"Is that all?"

He threw his hands up and gave an incredulous laugh. "Isn't it enough? Love is sweet incense, Detective, but revenge burns forever."

"All right," I said. "You're coming with us to the station to give a statement. Horner, take him in."

"Got it, Boss. You want to do this the hard way or the easy way?" he asked the Knave.

"Does the hard way involve handcuffs?" Knave asked.

"Usually."

Knave pulled a cigarette from his pocket and lit up. "No need for that." His words were a stream of smoke. "I'll come peacefully."

Horner shot me a look. "See you there?"

"After I check to see if the Bears found anything."

"Let's go, Knave."

Horner and the Knave strode toward the station, carrying on a quiet conversation.

We'd finally caught a break in the case. After I checked in with the Bears, I'd track down Baa-baa and squeeze the truth out of him.

If Baa-baa told us who hired him for information on Cole, we'd know who attacked Chuck.

A cow crossed the moon. Another followed. Dark, rotund time-keepers signaling the end of one day and the beginning of the next.

With dusk heading toward dark, I'd need to get a move on. The streets were growing crowded as boys and girls came out to play. One group whooped, another group called, the first up a ladder, the other down the wall.

Around the next corner I heard a low bleating laugh.

Sheep. Or maybe one sheep in particular.

I eyeballed the dark alley. Perfect place for a trap.

Or perfect place for a crime.

I strode into the narrow space, another low bleat calling me deeper.

This was dangerous, and going into it alone was a stupid move. I needed to call in back up.

I turned but didn't get a step. Something walloped the back of my head so hard, I sawed off to dreamland before I even hit the ground.

CHAPTER 22

The dream wasn't wasting any time. I was in the meadow in front of the Dwarves' cottage. A stream to my right babbled off into the distance.

In front of me stood a skeleton.

"Well?" I asked.

"What?" he replied.

"You're my dream. Get on with it."

"Right. Of course." He cleared his throat and cocked his skull to one side. "You must find my leg!"

I sighed at the dramatic delivery. It was going to be one of those kinds of dreams. "Did you lose it around here?" I asked. "In this dream?"

"Someone stole it. My leg. My leg!" he moaned.

I glanced down. Sure enough, his shin bone was missing.

His shin bone wasn't any ordinary shin bone. It was what had been used to make the Bone Flute, a powerful magical object that could, in the right hands, rewrite the Book.

Skeleton or not, drama queen or not, he was reporting a crime.

"When did you last see it?"

He tipped his head the other way and had to hook his finger in his eye hole to set it back in place.

"Two mornings ago. It was attached to my knee bone, my knee bone connected to my thigh bone, my thigh bone connected to my hip bone, my hip bone—"

"—where were all your bones resting?" I interrupted before he sang his way through all two hundred and six.

"I was buried where the river runs through the woods." He pointed at the small stream.

The stream was near the property boundary between the Three Pigs' and Dwarves' land. It was the section of Tulgey Wood Snow White had finally granted to the Pigs.

Maybe getting their hooves on that land had meant something more than expansion to the Pigs. Maybe it had meant grave robbing one of the most powerful and forbidden items in Las Fables.

"When did you notice the bone had gone missing? Did you see anyone suspic—"

"The pig took it."

That was quick.

"All right," I said. There were plenty of pigs in town, but this might be the fastest crime I'd ever solved. "Can you describe the pig?"

"Four feet. Hooves. Round snout. Oh!"

I waited.

"Pig sized."

Great.

"Did you notice anything *unusual* about the pig?"

"No. Just a regular pig with a tattoo of a wolf on his arm."

I only knew one Pig with that tattoo. Bricks, the eldest of the Three. "Anything else?"

"You must return my leg before midnight tomorrow or the nightmare will begin."

"Nightmare?"

He shrugged. "I assume. It's not as if I can read the future. This is a dream, not a crystal ball."

"Swell. I'll look for your shin bone. Now let me out of this dream."

He gave me a hollow stare.

"I need to get back to the waking world if I'm going to fix this. How about you give me a hand?"

He pulled off his hand and offered it to me.

Real joker.

"Buddy, I just need something to snap me out of it."

"Ah, violent assistance," he said with a look in his eye sockets I didn't like. "My favorite."

"No—"

Too late. He pulled back his hand and swung for my head.

Those knuckle bones hit my jaw like bowling pins going down for a strike. I went down too.

I fell.

And fell.

Before I could brace for impact, I landed softly on my feet in front of the alleyway.

It was night now, ink-blot dark.

The crescent moon hung high in the sky and the street was quiet, no match girl, no boys and girls or gingerbread. I'd been out for several hours.

Damn dream magic.

Choices: Go out to Chuck Charming's crime scene and see if the Bears were still there this late, which was unlikely.

Go to the station and see if Horner and the Knave were still there this late. Also unlikely.

Go home.

I rubbed the back of my neck.

Third choice: Go to the Pigs and demand they hand over the Bone Flute they had probably stolen from the skeleton.

But if the Pigs got belligerent, I'd need a search

warrant, backup, and transport. I sighed. The Pigs were always belligerent.

Choice two it was: Horner, the Knave, and the station.

I made my way along dark cobbles to the Wishing Well in the center of town, then took the path toward the station, moonlight glazing the street in vanilla cream.

The break in the case was good. The Knave's confession of selling Cole's schedule to Black Sheep was our first solid lead.

I didn't know how the Pigs and the Bone Flute figured into all this. But if the Pigs had the Flute and got their hooves on the Book, they would be more powerful than the Goose herself.

They could rewrite every rhyme, control everything and everyone in Las Fables. With that power, they could change any citizen's story. No royal or judge could stop them. We'd dance to any tune they fiddled, and none of us, not a one, would remember who we'd been before.

Thankfully, the Book was in the Goose's Vault deep in the forest. The only one who had a key to the Vault was King Cole.

If he wouldn't allow the Book to be used to save Snow White from the Sins, I was certain he'd never turn it over to the Pigs.

But with one royal injured and the attacker still on

the loose, only a fool would bet the farm on Cole's heartless stubbornness to keep Las Fables safe.

I refused to be that fool.

I picked up the pace and jogged down the dark, sleepy streets of my city. Dread came sneaking, creeping through my bones.

Something bad was going to happen.

Something worse than we'd ever known.

And I had no idea what it was.

CHAPTER 23

I jogged up the steps, pushed open the station door, and nearly ran into Horner.

"Peter," he said. "I thought you'd gone home for the night."

"There's been a robbery." I took off my hat and strode to my office. The station was as quiet as a winter scarecrow, the desks empty. Horner and me were the only two Joes left.

"When?" Horner followed me. "Where? What?"

"Two mornings ago. Out by the Dwarves' place. The Bone Flute."

He whistled. "The Bone Flute. How did you even hear—no, better just tell me everything."

He sat in the empty chair, the desk between us, and pulled a notebook and pen out of his pocket.

I hung up my coat and sat.

"Heard about it in a dream." I rattled off a brief description of the event.

Horner sat back. "Well, damn. Why would the Pigs steal the Bone Flute when they have a new business? Everything is coming up aces for them. Why commit a crime?"

"Power? Blackmail? Money? Who knows what's on the Pigs' minds. Update me. Where do things stand?"

"Knave gave a full statement. Nothing more than he already told us. We doubled security at the castle. Chuck is holding steady but isn't awake yet. No luck finding Baa-baa."

I tapped a finger on the desk, thinking. "We need to track that sheep down. And talk to the Pigs about the Bone Flute. See if they squeal."

"On it, Boss," Horner said around a huge yawn.

"No. You're beat. Yeah, I am too," I said to his pointed look. "We can pick this up in the morning."

"You're going home?" He hadn't moved.

"Yes."

"To sleep in your bed?"

"Yes."

"And on the way you're not going to knock on the Pigs' doors and demand they hand over the Bone Flute they stole?"

"Allegedly stole," I said with a grin. He knew me too well. I never rested when there was a case to be solved.

"Peter."

I spread my hands. "Fine. I'll go home and get some sleep. See you here at daybreak?"

"See you at daybreak," he agreed. He stood, waved as he yawned, and made his way through the station.

I sat for an extra minute or two, fighting the urge to go back on my word and stop by the Pigs' houses.

But it had been a long day on the heels of another long day. I was dead tired.

I pushed up onto my feet, gathered my coat and jacket, and found my way home.

The sun cracked the horizon and oozed across the land. A cock gave a lusty crow about dames losing shoes and masters without their fiddling sticks.

I was already on the way to the station.

The streets were noisy, good citizens of Las Fables hustling and bustling. Someone was warming up to sing for their supper though the meal was hours off.

In the distance, a choir of babies cried gently in the treetops.

The ball was tonight. Excitement rode the air like a silent bell ding-a-ling-a-linging through the city.

I took the stairs two at a time and pushed into the station.

The joint was already hopping, the entire force working like they'd put on their red shoes for dancing today.

"Peter," Horner called from his desk.

I detoured to him. "What you got?"

"Muffet found Baa-baa. He was delivering a bag of wool to the Little Boy down the lane."

"She bring him in for questioning?"

"Yep. Came peacefully, too."

I made a quick stop at the coffee machine and filled a cup. Not as good as Rip's but not bad. "Any other updates?"

"I contacted the Pigs. They said if we want to talk—about anything—they want their lawyers there."

"So, you're going to contact their lawyers and make sure they're there."

"Way ahead of you."

"When's the meeting with the Pigs?"

"In a couple hours."

That was good. It'd give us enough time to get info out of Baa-baa, then talk to the Pigs, then handle the royal ball.

"Good work, Horner."

"What a good boy am I," he said with a shrug. "Story and duty."

"Story and duty," I repeated, even though it felt like sand when I said it.

Was there more to life than story and duty? Should there be?

I made my way back to the interrogation room and found Muffet waiting outside the door.

"Muffet."

"Morning, Boss. You get any sleep?"

"Forty-one winks." I slurped coffee. "You got a smoke?"

"Sure." She dug in her pocket and produced a thin black cigarette. Her brand, not mine.

"Not my usual," I said.

"Straying outside the lines keeps things interesting, right?"

She held the cigarette between her lips and flicked a match to life. She took a long slow drag on the cigarette, exhaled smoke.

Then she flashed me a smile and turned the cigarette around in her fingers. She held it to my mouth.

I reached up. Our fingers touched. Her skin was silken soft.

I couldn't look away from her, didn't want to move an inch. But I put the cigarette to my mouth and inhaled.

The paper and smoke left a pleasant cinnamon burn on the inside of my mouth. I wondered where the cinnamon flavor came from. Muffet's lips, red, soft, curved in a sultry smile. I'd lay even money that if I kissed her, she'd taste like cinnamon.

Mercy.

"Well?" Her eyes held a mix of humor and challenge I found hard to resist.

"It's not so bad outside the lines."

She smirked, pleased with herself, then jerked her thumb toward the interrogation room. "Ready?"

"Or not. Let's get this done."

"Who hired you, Baa-baa?" Muffet repeated. "That's all we need to know."

We'd been at it for an hour. The sheep was still trying to pull the wool over our eyes.

"Three bags," Baa-baa said in his timid little voice. "Full. All of them full. No half bags, no quarter bags, no empty bags. Three. Full." He stared at the ceiling and his ears hung low and wobbled to and fro. "Bags."

He'd been saying that or a version of it like the song that never ends.

Muffet leaned back in her chair across the table from the wooly airhead and crossed her arms over her chest. "Who hired you to get Cole's schedule?"

"Not one a penny. Not two a penny..."

"All right," I said. "Baa-baa, you can go."

The sheep stopped mid-count and blinked at me. "Bags full," he said.

I moved to the door. "Thank you for your time. You may go now."

Baa-baa looked at the door, looked at Muffet, then back at me. "Go?" he asked in his little voice. "Where?"

"Meadow, lane, anywhere you want," I said. "We appreciate you coming in today."

"But...but..." He narrowed his eyes and his voice turned low and strong. "What's gonna happen to me if I leave?"

I shrugged. "Who knows? You sold out to someone who tried to off the Prince. We know it. They probably know we know it.

"That's not good for you. Not good at all. But one thing's for sure," I went on, "you sure do keep bad company for a sheep with no protection."

He sniffed. "Let me guess. You're going to offer me protection? Follow me everywhere. Threaten me unless I do what you want."

"Nope."

"But you just said..."

"I said thank you for coming in today."

His gaze zigged and zagged. Muffet, the door, me. Making choices. Did he want to bet on us keeping him safe, or was he putting it all on the person who hired him to deal dirt on the King?

"A witch," he said.

"Which witch?" Muffet asked.

"I want protection." He sat back and tapped his little hooves together.

"If you promise to take the stand and testify," I said, "we'll provide you with protection."

The sheep thought it over. I leaned against the wall like I had all day. Muffet pulled another cigarette and lit up, cinnamon smoke curling in the air.

Time *ticked*. Time *tocked*.

"Done," he said. "I'll take the stand. It was a witch in black." Baa-baa looked around the room with panic, like he expected the old girl to appear.

"All witches wear black," I said.

"Most," Muffet corrected.

"Most," I agreed. "Is there anything else about the witch that could identify her?"

"She wore a witch's hat. Big brim. Pointy at the top."

I gave him a hard stare.

"Fine. She wore a green necklace. This jewel as big as my hoof." He clenched his hoof to illustrate. "I could get a pretty price for that. And the little pies she made! Sweet, mouthwatering, tart..."

I didn't know about pies, but I'd seen the witch in black who wore a green necklace. She'd been at Mallberry's negotiating land rights with the Pigs right before the Prince had been attacked.

Time to knock on every hut and cottage in what was left of the Woods. Time to find that witch.

Muffet and I handed Baa-Baa over to Tom Stout. He'd work out a rotation of officers to check on the snitch of a sheep to make sure he was safe.

"The witch wants Cole dead?" Muffet asked, stopping at her desk to pick up her coat and extra bug spray. "You think she's the one behind Chuck's attack?"

"Foster said it was a magical wound. One he'd never seen before." I ducked into my office for my coat and hat. "Strange magic is a witch's bailiwick."

"But why? What do the witches get out of the King's death?"

"I don't know," I said. "Land? They were angry at the Pigs for mowing down the Tulgey Wood."

"Something isn't adding up, Boss."

I was about to ask her to do the math again when the door burst open, and the Knave stumbled through.

"The Book!" he gasped, wild-eyed and shaking. "The Book is missing!"

CHAPTER 24

The Knave paced outside my office. "It wasn't there. It wasn't there."

Horner, Muffet and I hadn't bothered to make him sit. We needed facts, fast.

"Start from the beginning," Horner said. "What were you doing at the Goose's Vault?"

"The King—King Cole—sent me for it. For the Book. He wanted to display it at the ball tonight. Wanted to read Snow White and Prince Charming's story to all assembled."

It was a power move to show off who had control over the Book. It sounded like something Cole would do.

"He gave you the key to the Vault?" Muffet asked.

"Yes. I..." He patted his pocket and produced the royal key. "I still have it."

"Did you unlock the Vault?" I asked.

"No. It was…the Vault door was broken. Torn off. Torn like paper."

We were silent.

He stopped pacing and wiped his hand over his face. "I know it sounds impossible. Like something out of a Nary Tale. But it's true. You can… You can go there and see. It is ripped away."

I called Tom Stout over to us. "Send the Bears to check out the Goose's Vault," I said. "Fingerprints, footprints, hoofprints, anything they can find."

"Got it, Boss." He hurried off.

"Does the King know?" I asked.

The Knave stopped pacing and gave a short, desperate laugh. "No. He'd destroy me. I didn't—I came here. Reported the crime." He swallowed. "He'll be expecting me back. He doesn't like the key to be out of his sight for long."

"I'll send an officer with you," I said. I held my hand up for Stout again, and he jogged over.

"Bears are on their way to the Vault," he reported.

"Good man," I said. "Escort the Knave back to the castle. We expect Cole to be angry. Keep the situation cool."

Tom gave me a winning smile. "Can do. Knave?" He waved his hand toward the door and the two of them started that way, the Knave's pace evening out after a few steps.

"Do you believe that story?" Muffet asked.

"Do you?" I asked.

She nodded. Horner nodded. "That makes three of us," I said.

"Go to the Vault?" Horner asked.

"Hit the streets looking for the Book?" Muffet suggested.

"Split up," I said. "Do both."

The door slammed open.

This little piggy—Straw—rushed into the station. This other little piggy—Sticks—trotted in behind him.

The last little piggy—Bricks—sauntered in like he owned the place. He belched and scratched at the scar that ran from the top of his ear, all the way home.

"We came here to report a crime," Sticks said.

"We're the victims," Straw whined.

"That's right," Bricks bellowed. "We're the victims here. Property that is rightfully ours was stolen."

I looked around the station to assign someone else to this case, but the place had emptied out. Every hand on deck was working security at the castle.

"Horner?" I asked.

"Got it, Boss." He walked to the Pigs. "Where are your lawyers?"

"We don't need no stinking lawyers to report a crime," Bricks said.

"All right," Horner tipped his chin. "Come on over

to my desk. I need all the information you can give me."

"So, you want Vault or streets?" Muffet asked me.

With how quickly she'd run down Baa-baa, I figured she was going to be better on the street than me. "Vault."

Her smile was bright. "Good. I need to stretch my legs anyway."

"Report back on the hour," I said.

She gave a short salute and started toward the doors.

"Peter," Horner called out. "You need to hear this."

"Can it wait?" If we were going to find the Book, or that witch, every second counted.

"It's important."

I strode to his desk.

"Bricks," Horner said. "Tell him."

"The Flute," he said, "which is *rightfully ours*, found on our land, that is *rightfully ours*, is gone."

"Flute?" I asked. Then it clicked.

"Bone Flute," Sticks said.

"Our Flute," Straw squeaked.

"You had the Flute?" I held up a finger. "No. Why did you have the Flute?"

"Because it's ours," Bricks grunted. "We just told you that."

"How did you get your hands on it? Who gave it to you?"

"No one," Straw said.

"We found it," Sticks added.

"Dug up when we cleared the Wood for Mallberry's," Bricks said with a shrug. "Put it in our safe to keep it, you know, safe."

"Who has access to your safe?"

"Just us," Bricks said.

"Just us," Sticks said.

"Just us," Straw squeaked. "And the witch."

We all stared at the smallest Pig who pressed his little hooves over his mouth.

"What did you do?" Bricks asked.

"What witch?" Horner asked.

"Straw?" Sticks pressed.

"She gave us treats!" Straw said. "Good pies. And she paid us money. You said we'd give her the Flute."

"I never said we'd give her the Flute," Bricks said. "We weren't going to give her the flute!"

"But the treats!" Straw insisted, as his brothers advanced on him, violence in their beady eyes.

"Hey," I shouted.

Three Pigs stared at me.

"Which witch did you give the Flute to?"

"The witch in black," Straw peeped.

"Green necklace?" I asked.

"How did you know?"

Horner gave me a look.

"Do you know her name?" I asked. "Where she lives? Who she bubbles and troubles with?"

"We don't know nothing about her," Bricks said, turning on his brothers again. "Which was why we weren't gonna hand over one of the most powerful magical items in Las Fables to her!"

"We know she bakes delicious little pies!" Straw said.

"*We* don't know that," Sticks said, "because you ate them all before we could have any!"

I gave a short whistle. "Shut it down," I commanded. "I don't care if you tear each other from trotter to snout. I just want to know who has the Flute. Do you understand?"

They were silent.

A flash of lightning flickered and was gone between one blink and the next.

I glanced out the window. The day was bright and cool. Not a cloud in the sky, which meant there couldn't be lightning.

Strange.

"Do you understand?" I repeated to the Pigs.

"Yes," the Pigs chorused, but their voices sounded wrong.

There were four. Four little pigs.

CHAPTER 25

I frowned. Four pigs?

Straw, Sticks, Bricks and...the last little piggy, the fourth, had me confused. I grappled to remember his name, then it came to me.

Stucco. The fourth little pig's name was Stucco. Big Bad had blown his house down right before he tried taking on Brick's fortress.

Right? Wasn't that how the story went? The Four Little Pigs and the Big Bad Wolf?

While it seemed correct, and I had proof of it standing in front of me, my gut said four wasn't correct. It was supposed to be something else. Some other number, some other combination.

Something was very, very wrong.

"Peter?" Horner asked, concern in his voice.

"File the paperwork," I said.

To the Pigs, I added, "You'll need to stay here and give Detective Horner all the information you have about your discovery of the Flute and its disappearance. Every detail you can remember."

The Pigs glanced at the piles of paperwork Horner was stacking on his desk.

"This gonna take some time?" Bricks asked.

"Yep," Horner said. "Hours."

"You don't need all of us to be here, do you?" Sticks asked.

"Every one of you. Have a seat, gentlepigs. Let's get this done."

"But the ball!" Stucco wailed.

"Shut up, Stucco," the other three Pigs shouted.

"The faster you all start answering questions, the better chance you'll have to catch the royal dessert course," Horner said.

The Pigs grumbled, but they each found a chair and sat. I gave Horner a look and he tilted his chin.

"I got this. Go see what you can find at the Vault."

The Vault. The stolen Book. Time to step on the gas.

I hurried out the door and down the stairs to the street.

The wind picked up, threading leaves into a string that it cracked-the-whipped into the sky.

I shivered and pawed my coat closer, making for the end of the block.

Las Fables was buzzing. Every lad, lass, horse, hound, cat, rat, and cow with the crumpled horn was out and about in their finery, chatting, shopping, primping, toasting.

The royal ball with the retelling of the Prince and Princess's love story spurred people to carry small boxes holding rings and trinkets and treats they intended to give their own loves.

It was good luck to vow love on a special day, and the royal celebration was the most special of all.

Consequently, love was everywhere—heady, thick, sweet as a hot candy shack in the summer.

The young posed and giggled, the sad smiled, and even old wives and old husbands shared glances with coy, inviting eyes.

The spell of fairytale love had knocked the entire citizenship of Las Fables senseless.

I made my way through the forget-ever-after, we're-living-happily-right-now crowd. The Three Blind Mice loitered at the corner of a building.

"Boys," I said as I made to cross the street.

"Good to see you, Peter," Hickory called out.

"Looking sharp, Detective," the second mouse, Dickory said. "Been working out?"

"Nice afternoon, isn't it?" the last mouse, Dock said calmly, his head tipped to the blue, blue sky.

I stopped, a chill washing down my spine. "You can see?"

Lightning flickered in the clear sky.

I rubbed my eyes and realized how stupid that question sounded. Of course they could see.

Three Kind Mice. That's how their story went, right?

Right, my head said.

Wrong, my gut said.

Thunder rolled above the far hills, distant, sleepy. Rip's bowler buddies inviting him to play a frame or two.

The first mouse, Hickory squinted up at me. "Sure we can see, Detective. Even though we're short, we've got great eyesight. Are you feeling okay?"

"Do you need to sit down?" Dickory asked.

"No, no." I cleared my throat. "I'm fine. Just fine. You boys take it easy."

"Sure thing!" Hickory called out.

"See you at the ball!" Dickory waved.

But Dock, the quiet one, scampered over to me and tapped his paw against my shiny shoe. Dock and I had some history. He'd always been the straight shooter in the group.

"Peter? A moment?"

I bent and held my hand out for him. He stepped onto my palm, and I stood.

"What do you need?" I asked.

"I think...no, I'm afraid something's wrong," he whispered. "I have memories. Memories of a carving knife and the Farmer's Wife. Memories of being in the dark, memories of a cane.

"I could walk this entire city with my eyes closed. I think I have done that before. For a long time maybe."

"Are those memories," I asked, "or a dream?"

Dock rested his warm paw on my thumb. "I think *this* is the dream, Peter. I think me seeing is a dream."

Thunder rolled. I had the urge to turn a slow circle, looking for the threat I couldn't name, but held my ground.

"If it is?" I asked.

"If it is," he said, "I don't want to ever wake up. This is the story I want to keep."

He patted my thumb, asking me to lower him back to the ground, so I did.

Dock scampered over to the other Mice, long tail, very obviously not cut off by a carving knife, swishing behind him. He gave me a wave.

"Thanks for listening, Peter," he called. "It *is* good to see you."

The other two Mice blew me kisses.

I watched the Three Kind Mice, saw how they ran, how they all ran off, happy.

Horner stepped out of the station, caught sight of me and jogged my way.

"What happened to the paperwork?" I asked.

"Something isn't adding up, Peter."

"Yeah," I said. "You seen the Mice lately?"

"Sure."

"Tell me the first line of their rhyme."

"Three Blind...wait. Three Kind Mice." He looked embarrassed to have forgotten their story. Only Horner, just like me, never forgot a story.

I started walking. He fell into step beside me. "What did you want to tell me?" I asked.

"It's the Pigs. Only three of them can remember the Bone Flute. Stucco swears he's never heard of it or the Book. That's strange, right?"

"It's strange. I think there's something seriously wrong, Horner."

"Wrong?"

"Peter!" Muffet yelled from down the block.

Horner and I rushed to her.

"It's Chuck," she said as soon as we were close. "He's awake. Doc Foster says Chuck knows who attacked him, and who stole the Book."

"How?" Horner asked.

"Who?" I asked.

"I don't know, and he wouldn't say. He wants to speak to you, Peter."

We turned as one and started toward the castle.

Around us, gingerbread men slowly crawled along. A little dog laughed—no, cried—to see such a sight.

The man in the moon came down too late and smacked his lips around hot peach porridge.

Georgie Porgie was getting kissed by a dry-eyed

pretty maid who sold sea smells down by the river where the bean stalk grows.

"Boss?" Muffet said.

Everything was off kilter. It was as if the entire town had see-sawed. We were all falling down, tumbling after, by the bushels full and sacks full.

"You see this, Peter?" Horner asked.

Cups running with forks, an entire herd of cows so flat footed they could never jump a fence, much less the moon, and white rabbits strolling as if they had all the time in the world.

"I see it," I said.

With each step, the oddness poked like a needle in the eye, then a moment later, it all seemed right, seem normal.

But my gut said this was wrong. All wrong.

Then it struck me.

I knew what was happening.

Someone, or some *thing*, was rewriting Las Fables.

CHAPTER 26

"Forsooth," Horner did cry. "Yonder looms the royal palace. Make haste to meet our beloved prince of charms!"

Horner's utterance so shocked me, my feet ceased their rhythm.

Horner and Muffet paused to tarry beside me.

"Pray, wilt thou speak thine unease?" Muffet queried.

"Fornications and expletives!" I exclaimed. "Canneth thou not perceive we are, even now, being rewritten?"

"Aye," Horner uttered.

"Verily," Muffet spake.

"Screweth this," said I. "Let us forwardeth, quicketh!"

And forwardeth did we most quick.

Within mine own thoughts did I consider the beastly rewriting we endured. Upon each breath, I struggled to remember what Las Fables and even what I, *myself*, had been just moments before.

The very thinking of those thoughts, old ghosts of memory clinging, irritated my weary head.

We came upon the great doors of the castle royal. A common guard greeted us and bade us follow through splendid corridors to the royal chambers, gilt in gold, encrusted in pearl and ruby, and draped in silk so fine a bolt of the same could be passed through Sir Thomas Thumb's pinky ring.

We entered the royal bed chambers of Charles the Charming. The Prince lay upon his bed, his awakened spirit casting pink across the pallor of his skin.

Gathered 'round him was the family majestic: His wife, raven-haired winter-skinned Snow White; the Queen, gloved in red silk to elbows, red hair loose about her shoulders, accentuating the queenly curve of bare shoulders; and the patriarch, King Cole.

"Peter," quoth Cole, golden and magnificent. "Hath thou cometh to bringeth me the head of the foe who hath so grievously wounded my son?"

"Nay—*no*," I growled. I had found the knowledge of our rewriting was made less elusive if I clung unto anger. And my cup did overfloweth with anger. "May I ask thy son a question?"

"Pray, speaketh unto him," Cole spoketh unto me.

I walkedeth toward the headeth of the bedeth utterly tiredeth of this shiteth.

Beyond the gilded shutters, the wind did rise. A soft whiffle tapped gently upon the pane, then was snuffed like silent sorrow. I strode toward the Prince.

While I walked there, barely blinking, my mind
filled with angry thinking,
Candles sent the shadows to stir curtains
draped down to the floor.
This sudden change in rhyme and deed,
brought me to Chuck's side with great speed,
And I asked him, "Kid, who did this,
who attacked you, I implore."
"Can you whisper, can you tell me,
who attacked you, I implore."
All Chuck did was softly snore.

His wife Snow White, fair and charming,
uttered this, her words alarming,
"He woke briefly speaking one word
that I've never heard before."
Here her voice did falter slightly,
and I touched her wrist, once, lightly,
Urging her to tell me, tell me,

what could chill her to her core.
"Fairest Princess, who fears nothing,
what word chills you to your core?"
All Chuck did was softly snore.

"I was dressing for the big night,
when I turned and saw his eyes bright,
"Deep, and looking at me with
the ghastly secret that he bore.
"He leaned forward, and my hand took,
horrid fear I saw in his look.
"All his strength and concentration,
in this one word did out pour.
"Then he whispered softly low: 'wock,' and his
strength it did out pour,
"Simply 'wock,' and nothing more."

Even though I am no scholar,
it was clear here, in the parlor,
That the royalty waited for me
to scoff at silly childhood lore.
But in the shadows of the night,
I'd heard the whiffles soft and light,
Nary Tales that reached out clutching,
catching at Las Fables' shore.
Perhaps the 'wock' that Chuck did speak
of drew upon Las Fables' shore:
Jabberwock, of monster lore.

Once again, the wind did call out,
moaning as I spoke in great doubt,
Told the royals, "Jabberwock
may be the culprit of Chuck's sore.
"But until I see its visage,
I will not accept the missive,
"That a monster is the danger
we must fight as if at war.
"Something roams the streets of our town
and rewrites our Book of lore."
All Chuck did was softly snore.

Then I turned to Muff and pal Jack,
"I must go and that's just the facts,
"To hunt the monster who has risen
from some nary childhood lore."
Horner shook his head and said low,
"Boss, you cannot face this strange foe,
Without me and Muff beside you—
we're your partners to the core."
Muffet smiled her slow and rare smile,
whis'pring "Boss, esprit de corps."
We as one, walked out the door.

CHAPTER 27

"Say, Pete," Horner drawled. "Where in tarnation are we going, anyways?"

We'd hightailed it out of the royals' hoity-toity digs to the dusty road outside. My first notion was to track down the Jabber-varmint's trail in the Woods where Chuck had been ambushed.

But the rewritin' was gettin' to be as annoying as a boot full of cactus.

"We need to rustle up the Book and hogtie the lowdown lily liver writing this chicken scratch."

This weren't the way this tale was supposed to be, and I intended to put an end to it, even if it meant a showdown at high noon.

We ran down that path like jalapeno gingerbread men—spittin' hot—and galloped the narrow trail that wound off to the Goose's Vault.

That's when Missy Muffet spoke up.

"Are you sure we're gonna find the scoundrel here, Boss? Seems to me that once a feller robs a joint, he don't linger around these parts. I say he already beat leather and skedaddled into the sunset."

I shot a look at her, and she fired one right back. We both reined it in, which put Horner a ways in front of us before he slowed up. We'd reached the fork in the trail.

Trail to the right would take us to where Chuck had been bushwhacked. Trail to the left rambled straight on to Goose's Vault where the Book had been stole.

"You got a better idea?" I asked Missy Muffet. "Go on. Keep the pot a-boiling."

Missy Muffet tipped her head. "I ain't got a better idea. 'Cept maybe we should split up. Cover the Vault. Cut a path to where Chuck chewed gravel."

"Naw, I don't reckon we should," I did reckon. "Someone's got ahold of the Book, and they're rewritin' Las Fables into hornswoggle and balderdash."

"And us, I suppose," Horner said, coming back to join in on the jawing. "Rewritin' us along with our tales."

That there was my fear. Leave it to my whip-smart partner to shovel up the root of the hassle. Not for the first time, I thanked my lucky stars he was my huckleberry.

Betwixt the three of us, I knew we was gonna save Las Fables.

I motioned us all on, and we legged it to where Chuck had been dry gulched. Didn't take long to make the scene.

"Give the area a gander and tell me if you see anything gone catawampus." I ducked under the sheriff's tape.

A small, child-like voice answered, "Okay, Mister."

I looked over at Horner, then down and down. Just a few paces from me was a bright-eyed little nipper wearing a sweater and knickers. He weren't but knee-high to a soda straw.

"Jack?" I whispered.

He showed off a gap-toothed grin. "I like hide-n-seek. What're we lookin' for?"

I blinked hard and my heart staggered.

"Jack," I asked, "how old are you?"

He held up one hand. "Five!"

My heart got up and fell down again. This was wrong. I remembered him as a growed-up man.

But his rhyme came to me: *Five-year-old Horner, sat in the corner*. Wasn't that right? Weren't he supposed to be just a little buckaroo?

Naw—*no*. I knew, deep in my gizzards that just minutes ago, he hadn't been a tyke.

I closed my eyes, straining to recollect what he had been, who he had been.

The evening wind howled, cold as an empty matchbox, sending chills across my hide.

"You okay, Mister?" he asked.

"We're being rewritten, Horner," I said. "This ain't the way we are."

"They have the Book," Missy Muffet said, holding her hand out for Jack. He walked over and took it.

"Yup," I agreed. "Who do you reckon has it?"

She shrugged and peered over my shoulder to the edge of the Wood. Sunlight was burning down to coals, shoveling fast into an ashy night.

"I reckon the rodents would say the Farmer's Wife, but I'm thinking it ain't her style."

"What about the Bone Flute?"

"Don't rightly know, Pete." She scowled, plumb tired of riddles that didn't have no answers. "There ain't any clue here. The wounds on Chuck weren't from no normal monster 'round town. If'n it's something else—"

"—the Jabberwock," I said.

"Right. The Jabberwock. It ain't here now, and it don't look like it ever came back after cleaning Chuck's clock."

"I don't like Nary Tales," Horner said, turning his head into Muffet's leg.

"Don't you worry now, little pardner," I said. "Things'll soon be fine as cream gravy."

The wind picked up.

I strained to hear a whiffle, a burble, but there was nothing 'cept the dusk in the tin sky above us, closing the lid on what was sure to be a cold, cold night.

So much had changed in Las Fables. I busted my thinker trying to figure the first change. The Dwarves' bloody murder?

Might have been the shuck, but it hadn't been the whole cob. Someone wanted what the Dwarves had—their land. And they'd wanted it for a reason.

"We better skedaddle," I said.

"We cutting dirt to Mallberry's?" Muffet asked.

"How'd you reckon?"

She shrugged. "The Jabberwock was in the Tulgey Wood. The same Wood the Pigs cut down. The same Wood the mall was built over and built out of. The same Wood where the Bone Flute was buried, dug up, locked away and stole. Weren't too hard to put two and two and two together."

"Let's hope your arithmetic adds up once we get there." I picked up Horner, and—

T'was the night of the big ball, and all through the
town,
all the creatures were clueless of what we had found.
The Book had been stolen by some sneaky foe,
The Bone Flute was missing, all this we did know.

From the rhyme of my thinking, my actions and deeds,
I knew we were surely still being deceived.
If we were to capture Prince Charming's attacker,
we must stop this horrible story-rhyme hacker.

Who was taking our words, our rhymes, and our city,
and grinding them down into tedious ditties.
We ran out past town, over long roads of gold brick,
While blankets of fog nestled down green-pea soup
thick.

Still on through the dark and the deep gloom of night,
my partners and I vowed to put all things right.
Now past huts, now past shacks, now past candy
condos,
to storefronts and diners and frogs in their pond-ohs.

To the top of the hill like three bats out of hell,
we dashed away, dashed away—dashed down to the
dell.
Wee Jack shuddered once, and tugged hard on my
sleeve,

"My end, Peter, has come. I think I must leave."

More quickly he faded, growin' light and then lighter.
"Hold on, pal," I told him while gripping him tighter.
With a shake of his head and through tears silver
bright,
"My story is gone, Pete. You must fight this rewrite."

Then his smile locked in rigor, his eyes sad and blue,
"Tell Blue that I love him, and you and Muff too."
Just a whisper he managed, "Esprit de corps, Boss."
Horner faded to nothing—was gone, ever lost.

To Muffet I turned, that sweet dame who I cared for.
She, too, was now fading, her face full of horror.
With her head held up high and her hands on her hips,
She said, "Give 'em hell, Boss," with a wink and a kiss.

She was gone, just like Horner, rewritten for good.
Both lost to the whims of a deranged, evil hood.
Angry mind and sore heart made me pull out my gun,
"This I swear to the Goose: I will get this job done."

CHAPTER 28

L as Fables paused. The dark city silent. Not a creature was stirring, except me. The sprawling mall ahead was empty as a lost pocket.

I ran down the cobble path through fog and dark of night. Neither snow nor rain nor heat nor gloom would keep me from saving our land.

Horner was gone. Muffet was gone.

This was bad. This was very bad.

I knew we could be rewritten, our stories, our lives. I knew with the right tools, and permissions, all of Las Fables could be rewritten. But a question I'd never asked myself suddenly filled my brain: Was there a way to erase the city?

Could someone erase everything we knew and

never write it back? Leave me—leave all of us—blank, wordless. As dead and forgotten as 'ol Gawking Ghoul?

Horner and Muffet might be gone, but they were counting on me. Las Fables was counting on me.

The odds of saving the land weren't good for a chump like me.

But then, I never listened to the odds.

I rounded the corner. In front of me was Mallberry's central courtyard. The stage where the Three—no Four—no *Three*—Pigs had stood was gone.

The fountain was still there, spraying dark, diamond-dusted water. In front of it loomed a beauty of a beast, two stories tall.

Not any old monster, this was *the* beast.

The Jabberwock.

Its eyes were twin furnaces stoked hot enough to catch the world on fire. A long, red-brown snout held jaws that bite. It's sinuous body was a wave of autumn-colored silk, wet feathers, glass beads, rippling as it swayed and breathed.

The claws that snatched held two things. In one claw was the Book—our Book, the most precious object in Las Fables—spread broken-spined across the creature's palm.

In the other was the Bone Flute, its magic blue ink pouring down and dripping off the sharpened point.

Drops of ink hit the page of the Book and hummed a do-re-me.

I stood there in uffish thought for several beats. Then I un-uffished myself.

This creature had rewritten Las Fables. It had erased Muffet, shrunk Jack, unblinded the Mice, and added an extra side of pork to the Little Pigs.

Now, I was going to take it down.

"Stop right there." I pulled my revolver.

"The jig is up. I am Detective Peter Peter. This is my city. Put your claws in the air. You are under arrest for rewriting rhymes without Goose or King."

Even with a gun pointed at its head, the monster didn't seem angry or frightened. No, it seemed sad.

The Jabberwock whiffled softly and swung the Bone Flute across the pages. Blue ink dripped and *sang*.

'Twas brillig, and the slithy toves,
Did gyre and gimble in the wabe:
All mimsy were the borogoves,
And the mome raths outgrabe.

The Jabberwock was writing itself into the Book.

"Freeze!" I yelled. The monster did not freeze. Its teeth snicker-snacked, and it burbled, the ink spreading.

Beware the Jabberwock, my son!
The jaws that bite, the claws that catch!

Beware the Jubjub bird, and shun
The frumious Bandersnatch!

I squeezed the trigger.

Three shots flew straight right on target, but the monster was nothing but thick smoke and flickering fire. Bullets passed through its head as easy as a boat row-rowing down a stream.

Then it opened massive jaws and spoke one nonsense word: "*Quee.*"

"Enough." I pulled out the handcuffs. I didn't know if they could hold the beast, but I'd find a way to make it work. "You're coming with me. You have the right to remain silent."

The Jabberwock tipped its head at an angle that wouldn't work if it had a spine. Then it thumbed through the Book.

"Wait!" I expected pages to tear. But the Jabberwock was careful with the paper.

It circled a page with magic blue ink, scratched out some words, wrote more in, then turned the Book so I could read it:

Jabberwock, Jabberwock, fly away home,
Thy Woods are torn down, thy children all gone.
All but one, on the Queen's red breast
That won't survive without a Tulgey nest.

That stopped me cold. If I was reading this right, the Jabberwock—the monster—was just a dame asking for help.

"You lost an egg?" I asked. "Your last egg?"

The monster nodded.

"You came to Las Fables because you need the Tulgey Wood for a nest?"

The nod again.

The Pigs cut down the Tulgey Wood. Even the part of it the Dwarves had vowed to keep safe. "Did the Pigs take your egg?"

The monster just stared, apparently unable to answer that question.

"So, you broke into the royal Vault and stole the Book." I glanced at its claws. They looked plenty strong enough to tear the Vault apart.

But something about this didn't sit right. I needed to one-two buckle these clues.

"Why attack Prince Charming? Why rewrite Las Fables when all you needed was to put your story in it? Were you planning to rewrite everything into a Tulgey Wood you would rule? Is that what you wanted?"

"No," a woman's voice said.

I turned. The Queen of Hearts strode into the courtyard. She wore black leather hunting breeches, boots, and jacket. Her copper hair was bound back so that the only color on her was the glowing green jewel —the Jabberwock's egg—hanging around her neck.

In one hand she carried a fine sword. She looked like she knew how to use it.

In the other she held a slim silver gun pointed at me.

She looked like she knew how to use that too.

CHAPTER 29

The Queen pointed her sword at the monster behind me.

"The Jabberwock didn't intend to hurt Charles," she said. "That was an accident. He was wearing the King's cloak and riding the King's horse."

"Cole should have been riding that day," I said, remembering the conversation with the King. "But how did she know...did you hire Baa-baa Black Sheep to get the King's schedule?"

"What else was I to do? Cole never trusted me with his schedule, or anything else. I did what I had to do."

"So, you hired the Sheep, knowing the Knave would take the bait and spill the beans. You wanted the King dead. Killed by a monster that shouldn't exist."

The Jabberwock made an offended sound.

"Isn't in the Book," I corrected.

The monster grumbled, mollified.

"Death wasn't the goal," the Queen said. "I wanted the keys to the Vault."

"You're telling me the monster attacked your son by accident?"

She shrugged, the ice in her eyes gone glacial, the gun still aimed at my chest. "Accidents happen to good men all the time, don't they, Detective Peter? I wouldn't have cared if he died."

"No, all you cared about is getting your hands on the Book."

"Yes, I want the Book! So I can live a life I don't despise. So I can free myself from a cruel man. My story will be *mine*, and this...this *prison* I've been enduring all these years...I will be free."

"What about the Knave?" I asked.

"Knave doesn't know anything." Her voice softened. "He doesn't deserve to be mixed up in this, not after what happened last time."

She was telling me some of the facts, but I needed the truth, just the truth to three-four shut this door.

"I'll buy that you were willing to rough up Cole to get the Book," I said. "But how did you get your hands on the Bone Flute?"

She scowled. "It's taken years. Little Miss Fairest in the Land refused to let anyone buy the Tulgey Wood from the Dwarves. I made generous offers, *very* generous offers. Enough that all Seven could have retired and never worked the mines again.

"But no. They argued about it. Most of them didn't want to sell, even though I am royalty. It is *my* land no matter how many little men are squatting on it."

Five-six, I was picking up sticks. The puzzle was coming together. "You paid the Old Woman to gun down the Dwarves."

"I did her a favor, she did me a favor."

I suddenly remembered the box in Chuck's hand when he walked into the Shoe Bar. The Queen's tarts. My gut twisted.

"She's doing hard time for a lousy box of tarts?"

The corner of her mouth lifted, but it was not a smile. "You haven't tried my tarts, Detective."

"Why would she give up everything for pie?"

"Desperate people give up everything for much less," she said.

Cold. This dame had it all figured out. If things went her way, there was nothing left to do but pour herself a drink and watch the world burn.

"Snow White was grieving and gave the Dwarves' corner of the Tulgey Wood to the Pigs," I said. "You didn't expect that did you?"

The ice cracked. "Filthy swine, building their filthy mall. They pulled strings and got to Snow before I could. That land should have been mine, *was* mine.

They didn't even know what they'd dug up, the idiots."

"And the Ball forced you to act."

"My timeline was...compressed."

"You had to stop the witches' protest before the Bone Flute was damaged, or worse, found by one of the other witches."

Her gaze sharpened. "You underestimate my standing among my sisters."

The events fell into place and I sorted them seven-eight and laid them straight.

The healing potions she'd given Chuck. The tarts that were so good, people would do whatever she asked them to do for them, give up their whole lives for them, give up the Bone Flute for them.

"You're a witch."

She cackled. "Of course I'm a witch. I'm the Queen."

A queen who had destroyed lives, stolen land, lied and cheated and gone into league with a Nary Tale monster who didn't belong in this city.

No, that last part was wrong. The Jabberwock might not have a story in the Book, but it needed a Tulgey Wood nest for its egg. Needed a home for its children.

Maybe it had nested here for many years, and we'd never noticed because it wasn't in the Book.

If so, and if the jewel around the Queen's neck

really was a Jabberwock egg, then she had forced the Jabberwock and its baby out of their habitat and toward extinction.

"You gave a monster the Book and let it rewrite our rhymes."

"That," she said, "is only temporary."

I leaned forward, ready to nine-ten, well, she wasn't a big fat hen, but I was all out of time for rhymes.

She sheathed her sword. "I wouldn't." She lifted the gun toward my head. "I am a very good shot. You," she ordered the Jabberwock like it was a doggy in the window. "Come."

The monster dissolved and reappeared next to her.

The Queen tapped the jewel resting on her chest. "Give it to me. Or else the egg is a scramble."

The Jabberwock's orange gaze focused on the jewel.

"Give it to me." She closed a fist around the egg and squeezed.

The Jabberwock burbled and held the Book out for the Queen.

"Very good." She released the egg and took the Book. "Now the Bone Flute."

The monster looked at me. Tears shimmered down her face like jeweled dust. She tipped her head, asking for something, pleading.

We didn't speak the same language, but somehow,

I had to convince her I was on her side. Somehow, I had to pull a Horner.

"What the Queen is doing is wrong," I said, laying out the truth just like my partner would. "As wrong as the Pigs cutting down the Tulgey Wood. I can give you a place for your nest. A safe place for your children."

The monster paused.

"Do not make me angry, Peter," the Queen said, "or I will off with your head!"

"Let me help you." I took a step toward the monster. That put me a step closer to the Queen too.

"I know you've done some bad things. Crimes. But I also know what it's like to be the only one left standing who can save the world. Save the people you care about."

The monster burbled a sob.

"Stop!" the Queen screamed.

"I can make sure justice is served and you are never treated this way again." I held my hand out for the Bone Flute. "Just give yourself up. Trust me. Please."

A shot rang out.

The punch in my shoulder bloomed white hot. I exhaled, and stumbled back. Sticks and stones might break my bones, but a bullet didn't feel all that great either.

"You have been in my way since the beginning," the Queen snarled. "I have worked too long and too hard to let a *nothing* story like you ruin it. I am going to enjoy erasing you."

She squeezed the trigger and another slug hit my chest. I dropped to my knees. "Don't," I begged the monster. "Don't give the Flute…"

The Queen was suddenly in front of the Jabberwock, sword drawn.

Eyes of flame, jaws that catch, claws that snatch.

The Jabberwock was as quick and nimble as a Jack. She roared, batting at the sword, snapping at the queen.

The monster was ferocious, but the Queen wasn't backing down. That dame was a skilled, ruthless swordswoman, even while holding the Book in one hand.

The magical sword snicker-snacked through the monster, leaving wounds that froze and shattered, taking parts of the monster with it.

The Jabberwock couldn't get in a good hit without the Queen twisting to put the fragile egg between them. The monster roared again—fury and frustration.

Then the Queen waved her sword like a wand and chanted a spell.

Things were about to go bad.

I braced my hand on the ground and geared up to jump into the fight.

The Jabberwock flicked a claw and knocked the Book from the Queen's grip.

The Queen gasped, tracking the Book's flight, her spell temporarily forgotten.

The Book flew end over end toward the fountain and skidded to a stop on the edge.

It teetered, it tottered, it dipped down toward the water.

The Book was not waterproof.

Things had just gone badder.

"You fool!" the Queen yelled.

But the Jabberwock was still roaring. It threw the Bone Flute in the opposite direction.

"No!" The Queen spun toward it...

I shouted and rushed her. She saw me, but it was too late.

We went down like a barrel full of nails, my arm twisting hard, the air rushing out of both our lungs as we hit the ground.

I got a hand around the jeweled egg and yanked. The chain broke and the egg came free.

The Queen kicked away, springing to her feet. I blinked hard, trying to get my bearings.

The Queen had lost her sword. She'd lost her gun. But she hadn't forgotten the spell. She chanted like her life depended on it.

I got to my knees.

She was angling toward the Book, her progress slowed by the Jabberwock's attack.

The monster appeared and disappeared around her, snapping in and out so quickly, it was like a swarm of Jabberwocks flying at her from every direction.

A wind picked up, gusting gustily.

The Book rocked. The Book slipped.

No.

I put all the pepper I had left in me into a sprint, and made one last desperate grab for the Book.

The Queen's hocus hit me with all her focus, and flattened me like someone had dropped a house.

I curled, keeping the egg safe from the spell. With my free hand, I stretched up, reaching for the Book.

My fingertips touched the spine.

Our Book, Las Fables' Book. The one thing that told us what we were, who we were. Our guiding light. Our sense of self.

Story and duty.

And it was me, with that single brush of my finger, who tipped it eevie, ivy, over the edge and sent the Book falling down and down.

It tumbled. It splashed. It sank.

I had failed.

I hadn't saved the world.

I'd ended it.

Just before everything went white, before the chilling cold of an ending I had never thought could happen wrapped around me, my gaze found the monster.

I opened my hand. Offering her the egg, the one small thing I had managed to do right.

The one small thing I had saved.

Then the world rub-a-dub-dubbed and went down the drain.

CHAPTER 30

"'Peter Peter Pumpkin Eater,'" a soft woman's voice said, "'had a wife, and couldn't keep her. Put her in a pumpkin shell, and there he kept her very well.' It's not my best effort, but it's not bad."

I woke with a gasp.

The wind was warm. I was damp as a cookie who'd hitched a river ride on the back of a clever fox.

The meadow around me was lavender green. A little stream chuckled through it.

An old woman sat in the grass beside me. Her striped-stockinged legs were stretched out in front of her. She had gold buckles on her shoes that would make Bobby Shafto jealous.

I'd never seen her before.

"Not the worst rhyme I've ever written I think I

was in the garden watching bugs when it came to me. I do like watching bugs."

"Who are you? Where am I?" I squinted to get a better look at her.

Her goose-white hair was long and thick. It winged behind her shoulders in a loose braid. Her face was round and dark. Her eyes small and bright behind wire-rimmed glasses.

"That's a lot of questions." There was mischief in her smile. "How are you feeling, Peter?"

I patted my shoulder, rubbed my chest. No blood. No holes. Nothing hurt.

"Good enough." I thought I might be in the company of royalty, but didn't know her name, her title.

I did, however, know that Las Fables was done for. "Is this the end?"

"Yes," the old woman said. "But the thing about endings? They are the best way to make new beginnings."

"So Las Fables is gone?"

"No, not at all. Well, not *exactly*."

She opened the picnic basket, pulled out a long thin bone and a red leather Book. The cover of the Book had two words embossed across it in gold: LAS FABLES.

Two words that meant the world to me. To a lot of people.

"The Book remains," she said. "Well—it will always remain." She patted it fondly. "But it is time for it to begin again."

She opened the Book and gathered the pages in one hand, letting them shuffle by, silent as a sea of dew.

Blank. Every page was blank.

"Tell me what you remember, Peter."

"I remember…" I chased the snips and snails of memories. "My partners, Muffet and Horner. My town, Las Fables. The Jabberwock monster. The Queen witch."

She nodded for me to go on.

"I don't remember you."

She seemed pleased. "That is because we haven't met yet. But you know who I am, don't you, Peter?"

Her voice tugged in my chest.

She was a soft palm on a cheek, a lullaby about pretty horses hummed on a gentle breeze. I knew who she was. Who she had to be.

"Mother Goose."

"Yes! Very good. You've always been clever. A little stubborn, but clever. I suppose it's why you became a detective. That and your desire for justice for all. Except for maybe that Chic Ken Little. He really gets your Billy goat!" She hooted, patting her leg in mirth.

"I don't like Chic," I said, "but I wouldn't stiff him. He'd get a fair trial if he had a run-in with the law."

"Oh, I know." She wiped under her eyes. "He just has a way of getting your goose. And I would know, I'm an expert on geese."

She nudged me with her elbow, cluing me in on her joke.

"I am also an expert on the stories in the Book," she said. "The stories that *used* to be in the Book."

Blank pages. The Book was nothing but blank pages.

My fingers had pushed the Book. I remembered that now. During the fight, I had knocked the Book into the water, and erased everything.

"Are all of them gone?" I asked.

"Every one."

"Dead," I whispered.

She hummed and her gaze followed a yellow butterfly looping high in the sky above us.

"Erased," she agreed. "But things can be done. There are actions you can take."

"Anything," I said. "I'll get it done."

"Excellent!" She shoved the Book and the Bone Flute at me. "Write it."

"Write what?" The Book and Bone Flute were lighter than I expected.

"Any of it. All of it."

"But...what if I don't remember the rhymes right? What if I change something, forget something, add something?"

Memories rolled through my head.

Muffet wearing that red dress and wishing for a different life. Wishing for a life in which she could choose who and what she wanted to be.

The Knave in black, forever in love and forever denied that love.

The Old Woman, broken and bitter, trading freedom for a life of solitude behind bars.

Even the Queen, driven by revenge and desperation.

So many stories and rhymes. So many tales locking us into what we were expected to be, punishing us when we stepped out of line.

"Do you think I got all the rhymes right when I wrote them?" Mother Goose asked.

She waited for an answer, long enough I finally met her gaze. My heart was pounding, but I told her the truth.

"No, Ma'am. You did not."

"So polite. But honest and correct. I did my best. I gave each of you a beginning. Wrote for you a Once Upon A Time. I never thought that would be all of it. I always hoped you'd each take a turn at writing your own story. Maybe take several turns."

There was a ringing in my ears. Shock, I thought, to hear such a thing, from the Mother.

"You wanted us to be different?"

"Why do you think the ink wasn't permanent?"

She asked. "Locking up the Book and only giving one person the key to it was not my best decision. But I have learned. See? Even my story can change."

"Yes, Ma'am," I said, not knowing what else I should say.

She leaned forward. "And *you* have learned."

"Yes, Ma'am."

"What have you learned, Peter Peter?"

"Stories change."

"Yes."

"People change."

"Often."

"And those who want to write their own story can. They should," I said.

She hummed. "Even monsters? Nary Tales?"

"I'm not the Fairest in the Land to make that decision."

"I'm not asking the Fairest in the Land. I'm asking you, Peter Peter. Do creatures who have never been in the Book deserve a place in it?"

I opened my mouth. All my life I'd been told no. Story and duty never changed.

But I wanted to say yes. Yes, of course. The Book could hold anything, anyone.

But that wasn't right either, was it? Me deciding a Nary Tale should be in the Book because I thought it should?

"If a Nary Tale wants to be, yes." I picked my way

through this new idea as uncertain as an itsy bitsy spider on a rainy day. "For as long as they want to be. When they don't want to be, then, no."

"Oh, Peter." Her eyes were star light, star bright. "I think the Book is in very good hands."

She stood and stretched arms up over head and shoulders, knees and toes, before putting fists to hips. "Well?"

I scrambled to my feet. "Yes, Ma'am?"

"Get to it."

She opened her hand in front of her mouth. There was a small, white goose feather in her palm. She blew the feather in my face.

I blinked.

She was gone.

CHAPTER 31

I opened the Book. The pages were blank as new fallen snow.

Near the middle, were two words written in her elegant hand: PETER PETER.

It was the beginning of my story. I had no idea what to write next.

A soft burble drew my attention.

The Jabberwock hovered down by the river where the green grass grows.

The monster was beautiful in her way, all the colors of autumn leaves. Her eyes burned with the warmth of a hearth. In her hand was a glowing green egg.

She burbled again, asking to come closer.

"As long as we're clear we aren't enemies," I said.

She lifted the egg before drawing it to her chest, her head tipped in question.

"I'll take that as agreement. Come on over."

Quick as a wink, the monster disappeared and reappeared in front of me. She showed me the egg again and leaned down. Her snout touched the top of my head.

A kiss. At least I hoped it was a kiss and not her trying to get a lick of me.

"Lay off the mushy stuff," I said. "I was just doing my job, Ma'am."

The monster folded like a summer scarf, compacting downward until she was about my height. She watched me with soft orange eyes.

I held up the Book. "You still want to nest in the Tulgey Wood?"

She nodded.

I opened the Book to a random page. "How do you want it to go?"

The monster whiffled and reached for the Bone Flute.

My gut reaction was to play keep away so the Bone Flute remained safe.

But Mother Goose was right. All that power in one person's hand had gotten us into this mess.

A new beginning meant doing things differently.

I gave the monster the Bone Flute and held the Book so she could write. "All yours."

The Jabberwock wrote her rhyme. It wasn't in a language I knew, but I somehow got the gist of it.

She had a home now in the Tulgey Wood. Her children would hatch and grow and thrive. They could leave it when they wanted, even for great stretches of time. But it would always be here for them, never destroyed.

It was short. To the point.

"Much less snicker-snacking than the original, but good," I said. "Happy, I think."

The monster burbled and gave me back the Bone Flute.

The Bone was warm. Ink glowed blue, singing like a sixpence song waiting for the birds.

I rested the tip of the Bone on the blank page next to the page with my rhyme.

I had no idea what to write.

Then it came to me. I wrote: Muffet. On the next page I wrote: Horner.

Blue ink sang into the stiff paper, then went quiet.

The ink was dry. Good. I turned the page, trying to think of who I should write next. If I were going to write every person into this thing, it was going to take days.

"I need a smoke," I muttered.

The click and hiss of a match made me glance up.

Horner, my partner, my companion, my friend, grinned that Horner grin.

He offered me a cigarette and a match. "Here you go, Peter."

"Horner!" I pushed the match and cigarette out of the way. I grabbed him in a hug and thumped him on the back.

He grunted from the impact, then laughed softly and returned the embrace.

"Jack," I said. "It's really good to see you."

"You too, Peter. You too."

"What does a gal have to do to get in on that action?" a familiar voice asked.

I leaned away from Horner.

Muffet smiled. "Hey, Boss."

"Muffet," I said, my voice rough.

Horner threw his arms wide. So, did I.

"Muffet!" he cheered.

She laughed and stepped up, put her left foot in, giving both of us a hug.

"So," she said as we all left-foot outted. "What's been going on?" She glanced at the Jabberwock. "Looks like I've missed a few things?"

"You can say that." I filled them in on the rewriting of Las Fables, the fight with the Queen, the Book being erased, and my meeting with the Goose herself.

"The way I see it," I said, "each of us should write our own story."

Horner whistled. Muffet held very still before a laugh burst free.

"Isn't that something?" she said. "Isn't that *something*?"

"It is." I offered her the Book and the Bone Flute. "Ladies first."

She took them and looked around. "I wish we had a table…"

The monster disappeared and reappeared with a table and chairs fit for royalty.

"Swell," Muffet said. "Thank you."

We all took a seat, the Book open in front of Muffet.

"Anything?" Her eyes twinkle twinkled like little stars.

"Even if it's the same as your old story."

She nodded, her shoulders dropping. Then she wrote.

The magic ink sang in blue, the kind of song that was uniquely Muffet. Soon, she set the Bone Flute down and stared at the page.

"That's it." She had written the spider out of her story, kept her job, and added her singing career. "Who's next?"

Horner lifted his finger. "I'll give it a go."

Horner didn't hesitate. He noted his story in his neat, precise writing, then grinned and spun the Book to me. He still had his job too, but there was no mention of pie in it. "Your turn, Peter."

I opened to the page where the Mother had

written my name. It felt huge, this responsibility. Defining my life for myself instead of being what others expected. "I don't think I'm ready yet."

"Sure, Boss," Muffet said. "Plenty of time to think it over."

"So, who's next?" Horner asked.

"Boy Blue?" I suggested.

The smile on Horner's face was a different kind of sugar and spice. It looked good on him. "Yes. Just Blue, though. So, he can choose."

I wrote Blue's name at the top of the page. As soon as the ink dried, Blue was standing in the meadow, blond hair shining in the sun.

"This is new." He sauntered over and sat next to Horner. "What's the deal?"

Horner filled him in. I pushed the Book and Bone Flute his way.

"Everyone?" Blue asked. "That's a lot of stories to get through."

"You got somewhere else you'd rather be?" Horner asked.

Blue laughed and bumped his shoulder into Horner's. "No, I like this just fine." He picked up the Bone Flute and got to writing, humming a tune about suede shoes not being stepped upon.

"Blue's right," Muffet whispered. "This is going to take a while."

"It can take until all the little piggies wee-wee-wee

their way home," I said, reaching for her hand. "Just so long as you're here. I want to spend the Once Upon, But Then One Day, and Happily Ever After with you, Muffet."

"For story and duty?" she asked.

"For life. All of it. Good days, bad rhymes, everything between the lines."

"Everything?" she asked.

"Everything," I promised.

She smiled, and I'd never seen a gal look so happy.

It took us hours. Hours to remember each Jack and Jill and boy with a beanstalk. But soon the Book was filled with hundreds of stories of cats, princesses, frogs and kings.

The fates of beasts and witches and wandering soldiers all came to life, along with riddles, rhymes, skipping songs, and wondrous tales.

We built up kingdoms and tore them down, turned frogs into princes, fish into prophets, and ducks into swans.

Some people, like Baa-baa, wrote their story back in the Book word-for-word the way it had been before. That sheep liked the life of crime and was sticking to it, all bags full.

I didn't want to do it, but eventually, I wrote Chic Ken Little into the Book.

"What a rube!" He snapped a shot, his camera point-blank in my face.

"This is your chance, Chic." I shoved the Bone Flute at him. "Write your story."

He stopped chewing gum and squinted at me. "What's the catch?"

"No catch," Horner said. "Whatever you want your life to be, write it. We're all starting out fresh as a fiddle here."

Chic took us in, trying to eye-spy the lie. Then he snatched up the Bone Flute and curved his arm around the page, blocking us from reading over his shoulder.

"There," he said, his skinny chest puffing up with pride. "I have a new name now. Dick."

A beat. A pause.

"Uh," Horner said. "Dick?"

"...Little. It's a manly name. No one's gonna make fun of me again!"

"But..." Blue looked at Horner, looked back at Chic. "Dick is sometimes slang for..."

"No, no," I said. "His story. His choice. Dick Little, right?"

There was a side of me, a side I probably shouldn't encourage, that wanted to call him Dick for the rest of his life.

"Dick Little," he agreed. "And I know what it's slang for, Blue."

"All right, then," Muffet said. "You're officially a Dick."

Blue brayed a startled laugh, and I coughed, but wasn't fooling anybody. Even Horner sniggered.

Dick ignored us all and snapped a couple shots of the Jabberwock. She bared her teeth and growled. He, smartly, turned tail and ran for town.

Then we gave the Queen and Knave their chance at the Book.

The Queen gave up her royalty, writing instead her story of being a master sword fighter and a witch, who was also a teacher.

"I've learned a lot," she said. "Of the wrong ways to go about changing your life. I'd like to share that knowledge. Show other, better ways to set boundaries to get what one needs."

The Knave surprised me by writing himself in as the headmaster of a school. "A place for children to play, to learn," he said. "I've always loved children."

He surprised the Queen even more when he took her hand. "I'll need teachers. Would you consider the job? Swords and spells would be very popular classes."

She blushed as pink as a pretty maid in a row. "I'll consider it. Perhaps you'll take a class from me first. Make sure it's what you want."

"I will." Then, placing her hand through his bent arm and walking away with her, he said, "You always have been what I want."

The only one who was angry to discover everything had been rewritten was King Cole. But it turned out he wanted to get into tobacco imports, so he wrote himself into a new business.

"The money," he said. It was the first time I'd ever heard wonder in his voice. "Do you know how much money I'm going to make? I'll be rich as a king! No," he corrected with an evil gleam in his eye, "richer!"

The sun drifted down into lullaby colors and Las Fables bustled with life.

At a table outside Paddy's Diner—a breezy café with adventurous cuisine—the Seven Dwarves picked apart and backfilled their stories. A few wanted out of the mining business. They wanted to take up other pursuits. What those pursuits might be was still being (loudly) decided.

Luckily, Snow White (who was no longer a princess, but still a judge) was mediating the lively discussion. She looked happy. They all looked happy.

Las Fables was not as it had once been. No, it was new. It was uncertain.

But even the uncertainty made it better.

"We're done?" Muffet asked.

"Looks like it." Horner stood and stretched his back. Blue wrapped an arm around Horner's ribs.

"I think we could all use a drink," Blue said. "Blue Suede Shoe's open. Coming, Peter? Muffet?"

"Soon." I gestured to the Jabberwock watching us

with warm eyes. She was folded so her egg was hidden.

"I need to escort the Jabberwock to her nest."

"I'll come with you," Muffet said.

"Ready?" I asked the monster.

She burbled and unfolded slightly.

There, in the warm flame colors of her body, sat a miniature monster.

The little monster blinked tiny twin-furnace eyes and stretched like a river of greens and blues toward its mother's face. Their snouts touched, and then, in a wynken, blinken and nod, the monsters were gone.

Muffet laughed.

Just a little ways off, Blue made a cooing sound and said, "So cute." Horner said something to him, and Blue chuckled.

"Looks like the Jabberwocks are going to be just fine," I said to Muffet. "How about you? Buy you a drink?"

"You actually going to take a night off, Boss?"

"Thought I'd give it a try. I hear there's a new torch singer at Blue's Suede Shoe Bar. Hottest thing in town."

Muffet winked. "She's gonna blow your socks off."

We started walking, the pumpkin-colored sun casting plum shadows over Las Fables. A gentle whiffling, one low, one high called out on the breeze.

The Jabberwocks were singing.

"They sound happy," Muffet said, leaning her head on my shoulder.

"Happily ever after." I held her close.

The Jabberwocks' song faded, replaced by a soft jazz tune from the Suede Shoe Bar.

A little dog laughed. Dishes dashed down the street. Soon, cows would be launching into orbit. All the world seemed right again.

Most stories like this end with a heartbroken dame slow-stepping out of a cheap, dimly lit office, realizing what was left of her shattered world had been glued back together in all the wrong ways.

The granite-faced Jack who had solved the case, but never found justice, takes one last swig of booze, lights a smoke, and wanders the dark and lonely streets toward a home as empty as all of his tomorrows.

This story ends with a chump.

A chump who didn't save the day.

A chump who lost everything.

A chump who found a way to begin again.

That lucky chump has two of the best people in the world at his side: Jack Horner who is a partner like no other, and a gal named Muffet who makes every minute better.

I'm that lucky chump. My name's Detective Peter Peter. And this isn't how my story ends.

It's how it begins.

Want to read more from Devon?

Find her latest books and fun newsletter at her website: www.DevonMonk.com

A NOTE ON THIS BOOK

200 words, and not a single word more. That was the rule for the monthly short story contest. It was the 1990's and I was a new member of SWAP, the writing group that met at our local library.

I was shy, awkward, unpublished, and absolutely terrified to meet writers.

But the 200 word contest seemed friendly. Even better, it was mostly anonymous. The story would be read to the room by someone who was not the author, and a silent vote would be tallied.

First prize got whatever coins fell into the hat passed around that night—usually enough to buy a few stamps or maybe a ream of cheap paper.

But it wasn't about the prize money, it was about the writing. Specifically, my writing. Could I deliver a story someone would enjoy? Could I do it with such a tight word limit? I was about to find out.

I wrote BAR NONE, a 200 word (and not a single word more) short story about the Seven Dwarves being murdered in the Shoe Bar. It was read. People laughed. People voted.

I won!

I was shaking in my boots. It was the first time I'd had live feedback from writers and readers—and that feedback was "yes". It was the first time I'd been paid for my writing (four dollars!) It was the first time I thought I might actually be able to do this, to be a writer.

Over the next decade, I wrote a lot of short stories, and three of them were Peter Peter stories: one about Snow White and the seven Sins, one about Muffet and her singing career, and one about Peter's ex-wife Peggy Plain.

Then, in 2004, it was time to try my hand at novels.

Of course I went right back to my first success, Peter Peter. I pulled his stories together, rewrote them, fleshed out the world, added new people, new rhymes, new crimes. It grew to a hefty 86,000 words, and I was proud of it, (even though it was unevenly written, and tended to wander) because it was the first fantasy novel I'd finished.

I pitched that book to an agent and she signed me.

She loved it, and sent it off to publishers. I was so convinced it would sell, (oh, past Devon, so naïve), I started writing a second novel.

And then the crushing news: no one wanted the book. "Books like this don't sell—nobody wants to read them." They wanted this new thing called urban fantasy, and would I write a book like that? (I did. It became my Allie Beckstrom series).

Peter Peter, and NURSERY CRIMES went into a drawer and stayed there for another seventeen years. I'd open the manuscript once in a while and try to figure out how to make it shine as a book, but I could never unlock its riddles: How funny should it be? How silly? How serious? How much mystery? How much angst?

In 2023, two things happened at once: I decided to start a Patreon, and my dearest friend who I met all those years ago at SWAP told me I better publish the Peter Peter book before she died (she wasn't ill, just delightfully demanding.)

So I went back to Peter Peter's roots, and rewrote the book into a tight, hard-boiled/noir detective mystery that also happened to be funny. I cut out half the original book (the boring half) and whittled it down to short, punchy chapters with a kick.

Those (still rough) chapters, were shared on my Patreon. And then...well, then I didn't know what to do with it. *"Books like this don't sell—nobody wants to read them."* And that was that, right?

Wrong. I still owed the book to my dear friend. It took me three more rewrites to finally have something I wanted to share with her. And that is this book, NURSERY CRIMES.

This story, these people, Peter Peter himself is, in so many ways, the beginning of my entire writing career. I may not have tried writing short stories if I hadn't written BAR NONE. I may not have ever written the Allie Beckstrom novels, if I hadn't pitched NURSERY CRIMES to that agent, and if she hadn't sent it out to publishers.

This is a special book for me, a book of the heart, as they say. My goal has always been to do it justice, to give Peter, Muffet, Horner and all the rest of the citizens of Las Fables a fair shake. To tell their stories, to let them tell their truths.

I hope I've done so. I can say at last, that stories like this don't always start out with a nervous dame walking into a room full of strangers, a 200 word story about dwarves and murder knocking around in her head, and a pile of cash on the line. But my story does. My name's Devon Monk, and this is my Once Upon A Time.

ACKNOWLEDGMENTS

This story began decades ago and has been helped along by so many people it will be hard to name them all.

To my siblings and family who read the Peter Peter short stories over the years and laughed at them, thank you! You encouraged me so much when I was just starting out, and continue to encourage me to this day. You're the best!

To my husband Russ, and my kids, Kameron and Mike, Konner and Anna (and Phoebe!) thank you for letting me be a part of your lives. You are the most wonderful part of mine. I love you all.

A special thank you goes out to Sharon Elaine Thompson. I would not have published this book without you telling me I must. You are a gift, my friend.

Thank you also to the talented artist Elyon/Caroline Léger for the lovely cover, and one more thank-you to Sharon Elaine Thompson, for the excellent copy edit and thoughtful suggestions that made this book even better.

To my Patreon supporters: This book came to be because you provided me with the space to share it. Thank you!

Big shout out to my super readers/super Patreon supporters: Amysue Chase, Aleta Goin, TJ Thorton, and Ann Tisdale. You rock!

Thank you also to: Salem Writers and Publishers, the Wordos, and the editors who first published the Peter Peter short stories. Your faith in Las Fables just made me want to write more, and all these years later, I have.

And lastly, thank you, dear reader for picking this up, and for giving this story a try. I hope you have enjoyed your visit to Las Fables and will come back to visit again soon!

About the Author

Devon Monk is a USA Today bestselling fantasy author. Her series include Ordinary Magic, Souls of the Road, West Hell Magic, House Immortal, Allie Beckstrom, Broken Magic, and the Age of Steam steampunk series. Her short fiction can be found in various anthologies and in her collection: A Cup of Normal.

Devon lives in lovely, rainy Oregon. When not writing, she is drinking too much coffee, watching hockey, or knitting ridiculous things.

Also by Devon Monk

SOULS OF THE ROAD

Wayward Souls

Wayward Moon

Wayward Sky

Wayward Devils

WAYWARD STORIES

Oak and Ink

LAS FABLES MYSTERY

Nursery Crimes

ORDINARY MAGIC

Death and Relaxation

Devils and Details

Gods and Ends

Rock Paper Scissors

Dime a Demon

Hell's Spells

Sealed with a Tryst

At Death's Door

Nobody's Ghoul

Brute of All Evil

WEST HELL MAGIC

Hazard

Spark

Graves

BROKEN MAGIC

Hell Bent

Stone Cold

Backlash

Dirty Work

HOUSE IMMORTAL

House Immortal

Infinity Bell

Crucible Zero

AGE OF STEAM

Dead Iron

Tin Swift

Cold Copper

Hang Fire (short story)

www.ingramcontent.com/pod-product-compliance
Lightning Source LLC
Chambersburg PA
CBHW070625170726
48291CB00003B/887